CW00393361

WHISTLING
IN THE
DARK

Also by the author

Hero on a Bicycle

WHISTLING
IN THE
DARK

A NOVEL BY

Shirley Hughes

**WALKER
BOOKS**

First published 2015 by Walker Books Ltd
87 Vauxhall Walk, London SE11 5HJ

2 4 6 8 10 9 7 5 3 1

On the endpapers of this book is a photograph of a vertical aerial view
from 1,800 feet of the waterfront from the Pier Head to the Albert Dock,
and of the city east to Derby Square, showing the extensive bomb damage
to the commercial centre of Liverpool. The shell of the burnt out
customs shed is visible left centre.

This book has been typeset in Times

Printed and bound in Great Britain by Clays Ltd, St Ives plc

British Library Cataloguing in Publication Data:
a catalogue record for this book is available from the British Library

ISBN 978-1-4063-6029-5

www.walker.co.uk
www.whistlinginthedarkbook.com

For those brave men who served in the British Merchant Navy during the Second World War

FOREWORD

Like my earlier novel, *Hero on a Bicycle*, this story is set in the Second World War, but in a very different place: a suburb of Liverpool during the terrifying winter of 1940–41, when the city was relentlessly bombarded almost every night by Hitler's Nazi airforce, the Luftwaffe.

I was living there then, aged thirteen, so it was very easy for me to imagine what it was like for Joan, my fictional heroine, her mum, her older sister, Audrey, her brother, Brian, and her younger sister, Judy (who, like all younger sisters, can be a bit of a pain at times!). Their father was lost at sea while serving in the Merchant Navy, and the family are struggling on as best they can.

Wartime, when it was not frightening, could be very boring. There were no holidays – the seaside was covered with barbed wire and gun emplacements. Travel was discouraged unless absolutely necessary, and endless time was spent queuing for food. The rationing system was very fair but restrictive – just enough to keep everyone healthy. Luxuries like sweets were a rarity. Nice clothes and, worst of all, nylon stockings, were almost unobtainable. Except, of course, on the black market, which no patriotic person would have stooped to using.

All troublesome enough, but in *Whistling in the Dark*, everything is further complicated because Joan's mum is being courted by the pompous bore Captain Ronnie Harper Jones. None of the children, except Judy, can stand him. He is stationed locally and never seems to be short of much-coveted luxury food supplies.

Despite the war and trouble at home, Joan and her friends somehow manage to have a good time, going to the cinema (Blitz-allowing), collecting salvage with a handcart and listening to the radio.

It is into this scene that a mysterious man appears – first seen by Joan as a face at the window.

And a series of events unfold which emanate from Nazi-occupied Europe, where conditions make life in war-torn Britain look like a bed of roses.

But the real heroes of this story are the men of the Merchant Navy, who, like Joan's dad and Audrey's boyfriend, Dai, risked their lives to bring food and vital supplies across the icy U-boat-infested Atlantic Ocean and saved Britain from starvation and defeat. They were poorly paid and ill-armed to retaliate when they were attacked, and their bravery is one of the great heroic achievements of the Second World War.

Shirley Hughes

CHAPTER 1

Norh-west England, autumn 1940

> *"There'll always be an England*
> *While there's a country lane,*
> *Wherever there's a cottage small*
> *Beside a field of grain.*
> *There'll—"*

Joan Armitage snapped the radio off, bringing Vera Lynn's famous voice to an abrupt stop. That song was definitely *not* one of her favourites. She preferred the big American swing bands like Benny Goodman, Artie Shaw and Glenn Miller, which played really hot dance music. Anyway, it was especially irritating to hear Vera going on about cottages and fields of grain when there wasn't anything like that here in their suburb, near Liverpool, in north-west England. Now, in wartime, even the beach was full of barbed wire and heavy artillery gun emplacements.

Joan was supposed to be concentrating on her French homework. Mum was always telling her that you couldn't do school work properly with the radio on. But if you were the one who actually had to *do* the work, you knew better. Music lightened the load a bit.

Joan sighed and picked up the grammar book. No one else was home yet, so this was as good a time as any to get on with it. Her big sister, Audrey, was staying the night with her best friend, Pat, and Mum had taken Judy – the most annoying six-year-old on the planet – to a jumble sale in aid of the war effort. Joan's brother, Brian, who had a half hour bicycle ride back from the grammar school, wasn't in yet.

The sitting room at the back of the house was freezing cold, as usual. Mum might light the fire when she came in, but you weren't supposed to have any heating on until evening because coal was in short supply.

It was late in the afternoon, but Joan did not want to close the blackout curtains yet. Instead, she pulled her chair over to the window to catch the last of the daylight. It was very still outside. She could hear the gulls crying as they swooped and wheeled over the miles of shining estuary mud out beyond the golf course. It was a sad, insistent sound, like someone calling and calling and never being answered.

Joan's attention wandered. She found herself looking at her legs. She stuck them out straight in front of her. Clad in grey socks, pulled up to the knee, they looked as discouraging as ever. Audrey had lovely legs, which made Joan rather jealous. It was a huge advantage when you got called up for military service and wore uniform, as Audrey, who was seventeen, soon would be.

Audrey wanted to join the Women's Royal Naval Service (WRNS) because they wore those nifty double-breasted jackets with gold buttons, black stockings and jaunty sailor hats. Brian wanted to go into the Royal Navy too, when he was called up, although that wouldn't be for two more years. Mum, of course, was dead against it. She said the war would be over by then, anyway, but if he had to go, he should opt for something that offered a safe desk job – ordnance, or something like that.

Their dad had been a sailor – a wireless operator on a Merchant Navy oil tanker – and had travelled to and fro across the Atlantic to Canada and America. "Sparks" everyone had called him. "Sparky by name, sparky by nature," Mum used to say. She had often grumbled about him always coming and going, leaving the hard, boring job of looking after everything at home to her – and she had hated the permanent suitcase in the hall. But Joan could remember how there was always a bit of a party atmosphere when their dad was around. He made them all laugh, gave her rides on his back, and brought presents back for her – often things you couldn't buy in England.

He had been due on leave, and they had all been half expecting him to walk in through the front door on that terrible day when the telegram arrived. It said that the oil tanker he was on had caught fire in the mid-Atlantic and had gone down with all hands lost. The company sent its sincere sympathy.

After that day, Joan had sort of blanked out for quite a while. She could hardly remember anything about all those relatives dressed in black who turned up and sat in the front room to "pay their respects", whatever that meant. Or the lady none of them liked very much who came to look after them for a bit while Mum was too ill with sadness to manage. There remained only a few sharply defined pictures in Joan's head – such as when she ran out into the back garden, blocking her ears, so that she didn't have to hear the awful muffled gulping noise Mum made when she was crying. The sky then had been flushed with fiery red, menacing and cruel. In Joan's mind, it fused with a picture she had seen on a postcard – a painting of a ship on fire at sea – which had terrified her. It was by an artist called J. M. W. Turner. She had a good memory for paintings that impressed her. They stayed in her head.

If she was being really honest, she didn't miss Dad so much now. He had been like a nice extra in her life, all fun and excitement when he was on leave, but there had usually been a tinge of relief when he set off again and they all settled back into their peacefully humdrum routine. She still thought about him, of course, especially when she was in the front room, where there was the photograph of him looking handsome in his uniform on the mantelpiece.

Judy, who was only a baby when he was killed, could hardly remember him, and Audrey was good at getting on with her own life. Next to Mum, it was Brian who missed him the most.

It is a pity, Joan thought, *that Mum never wants to talk about Dad.* It was as though it gave her pain whenever his name was mentioned. They all would have liked to talk about things they'd done with him, and what he had been like when he was young, and all that stuff. But as soon as they brought up the subject, Mum's face settled into a sad expression and she fell silent.

All this had been before the war against Hitler had started. Now quite a few local families and girls Joan knew at school had lost a father or brother, killed in action. There was a bond between people who had also suffered that first sickening moment of opening the telegram and the long drawn-out misery that followed as the reality of their loss began to sink in.

The war news since the German occupation of France and the evacuation of the British forces at Dunkirk had been very bad. And then the bombing had begun in earnest. Almost every night when it got dark, the air-raid siren began its warning wail, telling everyone to take cover.

Mum said that if Britain was ever occupied by the Nazis, they would have to leave their home and everything in it, and try to get to Ireland. In the meantime, they would just have to get on with it, as everybody these days was being urged to do. "Your courage, your cheerfulness, your resolution will bring us victory!" as the slogan on the poster said, although this was easier said than done.

Joan stared hard at her grammar book, stretching her eyes wide in a futile attempt to force herself to concentrate. The light was getting too bad now to see properly. She was just wondering when Mum and Judy would come home so they could have tea when she heard a gentle sound coming from outside, quite close to the window. A faint, low whistle.

Joan sat very still, listening. The hairs on the back of her neck began to prickle. She had that feeling you get when you know someone is watching you. Slowly, Joan turned her head. Over her shoulder, very near to the glass, she saw the dark shape of a man looking in at her.

CHAPTER 2

Brian sped down the final homeward stretch, freewheeling, and then expertly swerved his bicycle through the front gate. He was easing his heavy satchel from his back when he saw a shaft of light coming from the front door and Joan standing there, on the top step.

"Shut the door, quick!" he called. "The air-raid warden'll get us fined if he sees us showing that light!"

Joan didn't answer. Brian went in, slammed the door behind them both and then slung his satchel on the floor. "I'm *so* hungry! Is Mum in?" Still no answer from Joan. Then he saw her white face. "What's up?"

Joan replied in a whisper. "It's a man. I saw a man,

staring in at me through the sitting-room window. Just now. He was right there in the garden."

"What? What man?"

"I don't know. He was just sort of peering in. So I pulled the curtains and put on the lights."

Brian slowly loosened his school tie. "Do you think he's still here, then?"

"I don't know. I'm glad you're back. Ought we to go and look?"

"Not me. Not likely! Have you locked the back door?"

"No! Oh, I didn't think of that!"

Together they scooted through the kitchen, past the place where Mum kept her cleaning things and did the washing, and down to the end of the passage. Brian turned the key in the back door and bolted it. Then he peeped out of the little larder window. It wasn't quite dark yet. A watery sun was just disappearing into a low belt of purple cloud.

"I can't see anyone," he said.

"He was there. He had a cap on."

"An army cap?"

"No, I don't think so. I couldn't see very well. Only his eyes, sort of staring."

"Are you sure you're not making this up?"

Joan flung herself away from him, near to tears. "Of course I'm not. I *told* you. I was doing my homework and I looked round and *there* he was."

"Well, he's not there now. At least, I don't think so."

But even Brian was relieved when they heard Mum's key in the lock.

Her reaction was briskly practical, as it always was when there was any kind of family crisis, but they noticed that her voice was a bit shaky. "The sitting-room window, was it? Well, he can't have been a paperboy or he would have rung the doorbell. You two stay here with Judy. I'll just go and have a look around."

"I'll come with you," Brian offered bravely.

Judy, left alone with Joan, set up a wail. "I want my *tea*! When are we having tea? We didn't get anything to eat at the jumble sale. What's Mum doing in the garden? It's nearly dark! Is there a horrid man out there?"

Joan was in no mood to comfort her. Together they watched from the window as Brian and Mum searched the garden in the dying light, looking behind bushes and all around the rustic arbour where a neglected garden seat swung and creaked in the wind. It wasn't a very big garden, so it didn't take them long. At the far end, beyond the rubbish heap, there was a fence with a gate that led directly onto the golf course.

"If there was someone nosing around, he probably went out that way," Mum said when she and Brian came back indoors. "Anyway, he's gone now. Let's light the fire and have a cup of tea."

Judy was already asleep, and Joan was brushing her teeth and getting ready for bed in the room they shared. She kept peering out of the window, worried that the man was still lurking around. By the next morning, when it was beginning to get light, Joan was feeling braver. As Mum cooked breakfast before school, she opened the back door and stepped outside. The fear of the previous night's events was now eclipsed by her anxiety about not having done her French homework.

Joan wandered out a little way into the garden, scuffing her feet on the wet grass. The old seat hung there, dripping with rainwater and swaying gently. She went up to it and absently gave it a push. As it creaked to and fro, she noticed some muddy footprints underneath, quite fresh in the dewy grass. It looked as though somebody had been there, maybe slept there, quite recently. Last night, perhaps? She shivered and hurried back inside to get ready for school.

CHAPTER 3

Joan was ten minutes late for school, but she managed to slip into her classroom just before the bell went for prayers. There was a new girl in the class, standing awkwardly beside Miss Sanderson's desk. She was not a local girl. She was wearing the school uniform – a long-sleeved blouse with a school tie and a pleated navy serge tunic – but there was something weird about her. Her clothes looked too big and hung off her thin frame, and her hair was screwed up into braids and wound tightly around her head. She stood there with her hands clasped in front of her and her eyes cast down, as though she was frightened to meet anyone's gaze and was already expecting to be bullied.

Miss Sanderson tapped her desk with a ruler for silence.

"Girls, before we go into prayers, I want you to meet Ania. She is Polish, and she is joining our class. Her English is not too good yet – although I hear you're working hard on it, aren't you, Ania? – but I know you will all welcome her and help her settle down as soon as possible. Ania, would you like to take the desk here at the front, next to Angela Travis? She will help to explain any of our rules that you don't understand. And, by the way, Ania won't be joining us for prayers."

Just then the bell rang, and most of the pupils stood up. School prayers were strictly for Church of England girls only. Catholic and Jewish girls remained behind in the classroom, taking the opportunity to gossip and catch up on unfinished homework. Ania stood still, looking at her feet. *Heaven help her,* thought Joan, *if she's got to sit in the desk next to Angela Travis.*

Angela was a great favourite with the teaching staff, but among the girls she was known as the Himmler of the Lower Fifth, named after Hitler's Gestapo chief, and for very good reason. She was an outwardly demure girl with neatly combed, slightly sandy-coloured hair, and her mother always managed to send her to school every day in a freshly ironed blouse. Angela had a way of lowering her eyes and whispering behind her hand about other people to her particular gang of friends, or rather, to those luckless girls who were too frightened not to be her friends in case they got whispered about too.

Angela and her gang usually waited until mid-morning break, when everyone was in the playground, before giving the signal to begin the daily victimization. This began with sniggering, meaningful looks and some very carefully judged and easily overheard personal insults. Then they closed in on their prey: pinching, hair-pulling and dragging her clothes awry. If they did not succeed in making a girl cry before the bell went for the end of break, they reckoned they had failed and would intensify their efforts during the next one.

Doreen, Joan's best friend, was one of the few girls in the class who didn't care a jot for Angela and her gang and treated them with offhand contempt.

That morning, when the bell went and they were all outside, Doreen strolled over to where Ania was standing on her own, marooned like a stag at bay, and tried to start some sort of conversation. She met with very little success. Ania's eyes widened with fright and she could hardly manage more than a few replies in broken English in a voice so low it was almost inaudible. But Doreen's support did the trick. Angela and company, who had been circling like vultures, could not summon the nerve to pounce with Doreen standing there and Joan hovering in the background. Ania was saved, for that day at least.

"You were great, sticking up for that new girl at break today," Joan said later that afternoon as she and Doreen ambled homewards together. She was not proud of the fact that she hadn't been able to do what Doreen had with such casual confidence. Deep down, Joan was a little afraid of Angela. She knew how capable she was of turning on anyone who protected an obvious loser.

"Oh, *that Angela*," Doreen said carelessly. "Classic Nazi bullying tactics. Angela and her lot would have no trouble getting themselves promoted in the Hitler Youth. Actually, I was talking to someone earlier who seemed to know something about Ania. Came here with lots of other refugee kids – on a

Kindertransport, I think – just before the war began. She's been shunted around from one temporary place to another ever since so hasn't managed to pick up much English. Both her parents are dead and they can't trace any other family. Now she's billeted with some old lady – I think her name is Miss Mellor – in Ashchurch Avenue."

"Don't envy her. It's one of those roads near the promenade – so quiet that it's a big event when a cat walks past. Nothing doing except a lot of curtain-twitching," Joan said.

"Yeah. Ania muttered something about Miss Mellor being very fussy and ultra houseproud. She likes Ania to be out of the way as much as possible, so she has to walk about on her own after school until it gets dark and then she's allowed to clock in for supper. After that, it's sitting with Miss Mellor in the front room, listening to the nine o'clock news on the radio, then lights out and off to bed."

"Poor her. Anyway, let's hope Angela will stay away from her now or she might wish she was back where she came from!"

CHAPTER 4

It was Saturday morning, and Joan was helping Audrey to paint her legs with gravy browning. This was a tricky, exacting business, demanding time and concentration. But as nylons and proper leg make-up were now almost unobtainable, gravy browning was the only solution. The problem with it was that it tended to run and turn streaky in wet weather. It had to be applied very evenly. Then, to achieve a perfect effect, a line was drawn at the back of each leg with an eyebrow pencil to imitate a stocking seam. This was Joan's job, although she wasn't very good at it. It was part of the elaborate preparation that Audrey was making for meeting Dai Davies that evening.

Dai was a Welsh boy who had grown up locally

and was now serving as a wireless operator in the Merchant Navy, as their dad had done. His ship was part of the Atlantic convoys that made the dangerous crossings to America and Russia, bringing back vital supplies of food and armaments to Britain. Now his ship had docked at Liverpool and he was home on leave.

All the family liked Dai, and they knew that he was very special to Audrey. Plenty of other boys wanted to go out with her, but Dai was the one she liked best; the one she wrote letters to when he was at sea, even if it was by no means certain that he would get them. This leave was something Audrey had looked forward to a lot. But Joan knew that Mum was worried about her getting into a steady relationship with Dai while she was still so young. Joan had heard Mum talking about how dangerous his life at sea was. *As if we needed to be reminded of that,* Joan thought.

At last, Joan sat back on her heels and surveyed her handiwork. Privately, although she did not dare say so, she thought that Audrey's legs might look better if they were left bare, despite the risk of goosebumps.

"Do you think this colour's gone too orange?"

Audrey asked anxiously, craning over backwards to examine herself critically in the mirror.

"Well, perhaps a bit. But it'll be dark, anyway, won't it?"

"Not indoors! We're going to a dance at the church hall." Audrey's dress – navy blue with polka dots and a white bow at the neck – was already ironed and back on its hanger. A bit summery for the time of year, but this dress was by far the most becoming she owned, especially when worn with her white slingback, wedge heels.

It was some days after the incident of the mysterious man in the back garden and as he had not made any kind of reappearance, the family had all begun to forget about him. They had other things to worry about. Their house was in a so-called "safe" area, removed from what was supposed to be immediate danger, but they could see the flares and searchlights raking the night sky and hear the terrifying explosions as the Luftwaffe's main target – the Liverpool docks – was relentlessly bombed.

Joan's family didn't go into the public air-raid shelter unless things got really bad. Nobody wanted to sit in a dark, cold, smelly place for hours at night, huddled in blankets and waiting for the all clear. Mum had put a mattress and some cushions into the big cupboard under the stairs, which was supposed to be the safest place if the house got a direct hit, but Joan preferred to risk it in the comfort of her own bed.

The local cinemas stayed open in spite of the Blitz, and there were still dances at the youth club and in church halls. The dance Audrey was going to tonight with Dai would have a live band – local boys playing piano, saxophone, clarinet and drums – and a glittering ball made of tiny mirrors that revolved overhead when the lights were low, reflecting myriad kaleidoscopic colours onto the dancers. This was a special event.

Joan had been to one or two young teenage hops down at the youth club, persuaded by her friend Doreen, but she hadn't enjoyed them much. With Audrey and Dai, it was different – they were really keen on each other. The youth-club dances were pretty boring. Joan hated having to stand about waiting for a boy to come over and ask her to dance. Often he wasn't even someone she especially liked. It wasn't much fun being sweatily squeezed up against Ross Jenks or Derek Williams as they wheeled you around the room, treading on your feet. Brian's appearances at these events were mysterious. He sometimes arrived late in the evening with a couple of school friends and stood in the doorway, looking sternly detached, but Joan had never yet seen him take to the dance floor.

Joan much preferred an outing to the pictures with Doreen, if Mum would let her go. They went to the early five-thirty show so as to be back at home before the air-raid warning went off.

American movies offered a glimpse of heaven compared with the chilly reality of the blackout and endless queues for the meagre family meat ration, or the mere possibility of a cake or a packet of biscuits.

The cinema was a magical place in which glamorous characters, played by stars such as Myrna Loy, Clark Gable or Katharine Hepburn, sat about in luxury penthouse apartments sipping cocktails as a waiter wheeled in a trolley laden with delicious food. A wonderful world in which the famous Judy Garland and Mickey Rooney sang and danced in an enviable whirl of bobby socks, high-school proms and romance. In this Hollywood paradise, girls had rooms of their own with elaborate flounced bedcovers and full-length mirrors, instead of having to share a cramped back bedroom with a maddening six-year-old.

Joan had noticed in the local paper that a really good Betty Grable film was showing at the Queensway Cinema that evening. She was longing to see it and was determined to get there if she could.

While Audrey was still fussing over her legs, the doorbell rang.

"Ross and Derek are here, Joanie," Mum called up the stairs. Joan had quite forgotten that it was her day to do youth-service work. She went down reluctantly. The children at Joan's school usually took it in turns to collect salvage for the war effort – saucepans, newspapers, bits of wood – all of which had to be kept separate. The metal stuff was the most important, or so they had been told. It was going to be melted down to make Spitfires.

"Come on, Joan, we're running late," Ross said impatiently. Ross had overdone the Brylcreem on his hair, as usual. It stood up in a high quiff over his forehead.

Derek remained impassive, leaning on the handles of the cart.

"OK, OK, I'm just coming," said Joan, struggling into her cardigan.

As soon as they got round the nearest corner and were heading for the seafront, Ross and Derek both produced cigarettes and lit up. Derek smoked in a way he hoped made him look sophisticated, holding it between thumb and second finger and puffing out smoke rings with half-closed eyes.

"We've got four left," he told Joan. "Want one? My dad's home on leave and we pinched them from his uniform pocket."

"No, thanks. I don't like them. Come on. Let's start with the posh houses down near the Royal Hotel."

The boys agreed that this was a good idea and the three set off, pushing the handcart at a brisk pace. Soon they had collected quite a haul, including half an old bicycle, a sack full of tin cans and many bundles of newspapers. One lady gave them a whole set of saucepans.

Feeling pleased with themselves, they trundled on down to the promenade. Here, a row of shelters with peaked roofs offered a view of the muddy Dee Estuary and an offshore island with its wireless mast and coastguard's house. Beyond it, across the incoming tide, lay the misty coast of North Wales. The front-facing seats of the shelters caught the full impact of a sharp sea breeze. The back ones, separated by a cracked, salt-caked glass window, were marginally less draughty. Joan knew that, in the evenings, the shelters offered some of the few available refuges for young servicemen, stationed locally and far from home, and their girlfriends. Now, though, they were deserted.

"Gee, I'm hungry," said Ross, slumping down on a seat and splaying out his long, spindly legs. "Do you remember when you could buy buns at that cafe by the outdoor swimming baths? And there was a Wall's ice-cream man with a tricycle on the prom?"

"'Stop me and buy one,'" said Derek dreamily, quoting from the ad on the ice-cream cart with a far-off look in his eye. "The snow-fruits were tuppence. They dripped down your arm. I can hardly remember what they tasted like now."

"Perhaps they'll give us a sandwich at the hotel, if we call there next," said Joan. "My mum helps there now and again and I know Basia and Gosia, two Polish ladies who work in the kitchen. Mum teaches them English sometimes."

The Royal Hotel loomed up over the boating lake like a many-chimneyed Gothic palace in a fairy tale. The great glass sun lounge was sealed off, leaving a riot of potted palms and tangled greenery rotting inside. All the other windows were criss-crossed with sticky tape to stop them from shattering inwards if there was a bomb blast.

The place no longer functioned as a hotel – no leisured guests or golf enthusiasts reclined on deckchairs on the terrace. The attic floors were completely closed up and the lower rooms had been commandeered to accommodate evacuee children from the danger areas in and around Liverpool.

Teams of hard-working volunteers from the Women's Voluntary Services now ran the place, aided by a motley collection of kitchen workers. As Joan and the boys approached the hotel, they could see a few ladies attempting to organize a ball game with the younger children on what used to be the hotel lawn, but it was rapidly descending into chaos.

Joan, Ross and Derek parked their laden handcart by the kitchen entrance. A row of older children, ranged along the doorstep like seagulls beadily eyeing a potential snack, regarded them with some hostility.

"You can't come in here," one girl said. "It's not dinnertime yet. We've got to stay out until the gong goes."

"We're collecting salvage," Joan told them.

"Aw, gerra way. There's no salvage here!"

Ross and Derek, who seemed to be rapidly losing interest in this whole salvage project, leaned wearily against the wall and stared into space.

"Are Basia and Gosia here?" Joan asked.

"Them two foreign women? Nah. They didn't show up today. Probably scared. I wouldn't hang around this place too often if I was you."

"Why not?"

"It's bloody haunted! Didn't you know? There's a ghost that walks in the attics at night – in the bit that's sealed off. We're sleeping in the rooms underneath and we hear it sometimes, creeping around. Boards squeaking, footsteps and that."

Ross and Derek had not moved, but Joan knew they had begun to listen intently.

"There can't be a ghost up there," she said. "It must be a person." And she stopped short, realizing as she said it that this seemed even scarier.

"Can't be!" said the girl firmly. "They'd be found

out. They'd need food and stuff. Ghosts don't need food. Anyway, nobody could get up there. It's a ghost, all right. It's dead scary. Especially at night with the blackout and all."

Later, as they pushed the handcart round to the WVS salvage collection centre, Ross and Derek were unusually quiet.

"She's talking rubbish, that kid," said Ross at last. "Those Liverpool kids'll believe anything." But he did not sound completely convinced.

CHAPTER 5

It was past noon by the time they had delivered the salvage to the WVS collection centre and returned the handcart, and they were aching with hunger. Ross and Derek, who seemed to have nothing better to do, mooched wearily along with Joan in the direction of her house. On the way, they ran into Doreen, looking lovely as usual: pink-faced, blonde hair blowing in the wind. The boys perked up considerably when they saw her, but she ignored them.

"Mummy says I can go to the pictures with you tonight if we catch the early show," she told Joan. "Can you call for me at my house at about five and we'll walk down to the Queensway together?"

"Great! They're showing *Down Argentine Way*

with Betty Grable. It's got that new singer in it – what's her name? Carmen Miranda – the one who wears the tutti-frutti hat!"

To show she knew who Joan meant, Doreen performed a few expert samba steps on the pavement. Even in flat lace-ups and ankle socks, her legs looked good. Ross and Derek exchanged glances. All three watched as Doreen tripped off, waving but not looking back. *Why do I have an older sister* and *a best friend with lovely legs?* Joan thought to herself.

"Will you be going?" she asked Ross, then wished she hadn't. She'd remembered too late that Ross's dad probably couldn't afford to give him money for the pictures on an army corporal's pay.

"Nah," Ross said scornfully. "I'm going to football practice. Can't stand all that daft dance stuff, anyway. Tutti-frutti rubbish."

"Me neither," agreed Derek and he did a terrible imitation of what he thought was Carmen Miranda's song and dance routine, flapping his hands about above his head.

"We like action pictures. John Wayne, James Cagney and that," said Ross. After crouching down low, he emptied the chambers of an imaginary pair of pistols into Derek, who staggered about, clutching his stomach before falling flat on the pavement.

Joan was greeted by the welcome smell of dinner cooking as she entered the house. Mum usually managed to stretch the rations to something good on Saturday. They all lived, ate, did homework and listened to the wireless in the back sitting room next to the kitchen, where it was warm. The front room was left cold and unheated, except for special occasions. But, with a sinking heart, Joan heard voices in there. This meant a visitor, and she was pretty sure who it was. She tried to sidle through the hall and get upstairs unnoticed, but her mum heard her and called out, "Is that you, Joanie? Come on in!"

Reluctantly Joan hovered in the doorway, still wearing her coat.

Captain Ronnie Harper Jones was leaning against the mantelpiece, warming his backside by the small fire that Mum must have been reckless enough to light in honour of his visit. She was sitting on the settee, wearing her best ice-blue twinset, with her hair carefully done up in front. On the table was a half-opened parcel full of goodies. Joan immediately

41

spotted a packet of butter and two bags of sugar, as well as what looked like some promising tinned goods. But she wouldn't let her eyes rest on them.

"Joanie!" cried Captain Harper Jones. "Been out helping the war effort, I hear! *Good* for you!"

Joan nodded but said nothing. Nobody called her Joanie except her family and sometimes Doreen. She didn't like someone she hardly knew doing it. Especially this man, with his carefully tended moustache and dapper army officer's uniform, with polished Sam Browne belt, gleaming brass buttons and three pips up on each shoulder.

Some people might find him pretty impressive (including, for some unknown reason, her mum), but in Joan's opinion, he was on the oily side. Anyway, his eyes were too close together. She wished he hadn't taken to dropping in so often, especially not at Saturday dinnertime. He was stationed locally with the Army Catering Corps – "the wonderfully whacky world of army supplies", as he laughingly called it. He was always explaining that he would have preferred to be with a crack commando unit, to see some real action "now the Jerry war was on the doorstep", but unfortunately he had failed his medical on account of his eyesight.

"Just dropped by to bring in a few extras for you," he said. "Help to eke out the rations!"

"It's awfully kind of you," said Mum. "We can manage, of course, but it's a bit difficult with all these hungry people around."

"Glad to help out any time. I've just come off parade. That's why I'm all spruced up in dress uniform. Got to set a good example and all that. I won't allow any laxity in *my* unit. I keep them up to scratch in the smartness department. And I see to it that the batman who looks after my uniform does a proper job with the spit and polish."

"We've just been discussing the big charity dinner dance that's coming up soon in aid of the Red Cross," said Mum. "Ronnie's doing all the catering for it."

"It's going to be at the golf club," he explained nonchalantly. "I'm a friend of the chap who chairs the committee. Promises to be a pretty swish affair – Blitz allowing, that is. I'm taking your mother, as a matter of fact, and I was just wondering if you'd like to join us?"

"I'd rather not," said Joan. "I'm not much good at ballroom dancing."

"Oh, come on, Joanie. You'd love it," said Mum. Joan shot her a look.

"Is Audrey going?" she asked.

"No. Dai will be back at sea by then and she doesn't want to dance with anyone but him. And you know how Brian feels about dances!"

"I haven't got anything to wear!" Joan protested.

"We'll find you something. Doreen and her brother will be there, I expect."

Joan felt trapped. She could hardly say she was doing something else that evening when Mum knew perfectly well that she wasn't.

"You'll be the belle of the ball!" Ronnie laughed. "That is, if your mother doesn't steal all the limelight."

Joan didn't bother to reply. She knew when she was defeated. She refused to catch Mum's eye. *If he stays for dinner, I'm not going to be polite to him,* she thought.

But not even the pushiest guests ever invited themselves over for a meal in these days of food rationing. As Ronnie prepared to go, there was a knock at the door. Mum answered it.

Two men in army uniform, a sergeant and a corporal, were standing on the doorstep. Joan could tell by the red bands around their caps that they were military policemen.

"Sorry to disturb you," said the sergeant, pushing his way past Mum without waiting to be invited in. He nodded to Ronnie. "We're looking for someone. We've got reason to believe he might be hanging around this area. Have you seen anyone suspicious at all?"

"Why? What's he done?" Mum asked.

"Deserter. A Polish chap. One of the refugees attached to the pioneer corps doing roadwork – digging ditches and that. Now he's gone absent without leave and we've got orders to arrest him on sight."

"I thought the Poles were meant to be on our side," said Mum.

"He's got no proper papers. On the loose illegally."

"Will that mean military prison?"

The sergeant gave her a sharp look. "Yes – probably."

"Military prison is the best place for him," Ronnie said.

"Have you seen him?" the sergeant asked Mum. "We think he's been hanging around here the last few nights."

"No. I've been at home all morning, and there's been nobody around here as far as I know."

"Your husband away in the services?"

"He was. Merchant Navy. I'm a widow."

The sergeant paused. His voice softened, but only slightly. "Sorry to hear it. Your neighbours at home?"

"Mr Roberts is probably out training with the Home Guard, but I think Mrs Roberts is at home."

"Well, lock and bolt all your doors carefully, and if you see anything or anyone suspicious, report it immediately."

"Yes, of course."

The sergeant saluted Mum and Ronnie and then motioned to the corporal to leave. Mum closed the door carefully. Soon they heard them hammering at the Roberts' front door.

"It's a very bad show to have these undesirables on the loose," said Ronnie. "The trouble is we've got too many of these European refugees and displaced persons over here now. Poles, Czechs, Jews – all sorts. A good many of them are safe and secure, interned on the Isle of Man, and a good thing too. I'm sympathetic, of course, but we've got to keep track of them."

"They've had a terrible time, most of them," said

Mum with some spirit. "We're fighting Hitler for what he's doing to them. The least we can do is to take some of them in."

"Yes, yes, of course, my dear. You're such a sweet, soft-hearted person, I knew you'd take that view. Just don't worry about it. Leave it to the Military Police. And you must report it right away if that deserter does show his face around here."

"Don't worry, I will."

Just then Judy emerged from the back room, putting on her "cute little girl" act, as usual.

"Ah! Here's my little Shirley Temple!" cried Ronnie, adjusting back to his usual jocularity. "Where have you been hiding, Judy? I'm just off, I'm afraid. But I've left a parcel for all of you – and there's a special packet of sweets just for you."

"Ooh, thanks, Captain Harper Jones."

"Ronnie," he said. "I want all you children to call me Ronnie."

"Thank you, Ronnie."

As the front door closed behind him, Brian appeared from the back room with a hunted expression. "Has he gone?"

Mum looked suddenly weary.

"Yes, he's gone. But I wish you could have come out to say goodbye at least, Brian."

"Not me. Not likely! Can't stand the bloke."

"*I* like him," said Judy. She had already taken control of the packet of sweets, but as Joan noticed bitterly, she wasn't offering them around.

"Mum, why did you lie to those policemen?" Joan asked. "Why didn't you tell them about that man who was in the garden a few nights ago?"

Mum walked off into the kitchen, saying nothing. Joan and Brian trailed after her and watched as she slammed saucepans about in the sink.

"I didn't want to put them onto him," she said finally. "That is, if the man they're looking for is the same one as you saw, Joanie."

"But they're the police!" said Brian. "Why ever not, Mum?"

"Well, if you must know, it's because I've heard about those military prisons – 'glasshouses', they call them. They're very, very tough. And if you're a foreigner of any kind in one of those places these days, heaven help you."

"Suppose he does come back?" asked Joan.

"Then I'll get the police onto him straight off, don't

worry. I just thought we might give him one chance to get away. The Poles are supposed to be on our side, after all. Look how bravely their airmen fought in the Battle of Britain. Now the whole of Warsaw's been destroyed and their country's occupied by the Nazis. For all we know, this chap may be some poor devil who's gone on the run because he just couldn't take it any more."

"But, Mum—"

"That's enough. Now come on, you two. Go and check on Judy for me. She'll ruin her dinner if she eats all those sweets."

CHAPTER 6

As soon as they had eaten midday dinner, Joan escaped, leaving Audrey to help Mum wash the dishes. She went upstairs to the landing, let down the ladder that led up to the attic and scrambled up. Hardly anyone went up there these days except her. She had managed to clear all the battered suitcases, full of moth-eaten clothes, assorted boxes of broken electrical equipment, old magazines and Christmas decorations across to one side to make room for what she liked to call her studio.

There was a skylight in the roof that let in quite a good light. She had arranged a chair and a folding table on which she had set out her watercolour paint box, pencil case, and jar that held her precious brushes

– good ones, proper sable. These, together with a big art folder and a block of watercolour paper, were a gift from a neighbour who had enthusiastically taken up art lessons but soon given them up.

Joan did art at school, of course, every Friday afternoon with the highly strung Miss Burrows, who wore hand-embroidered smocks and was very keen on arranging a tasteful vase of spring flowers or autumn leaves (depending on the season) for them to paint. Most girls in the class had long since given up any serious attempt to rise to this challenge, and sat chatting at the back of the room while occasionally dabbing a bit of colour here and there. Joan made what she could of it. Art was one of the few subjects in which she regularly got an *A*. But she didn't enjoy it much, not at school.

For Joan, the real stuff was up here in the attic. This was where she came to draw comic strips, fashion drawings, cartoons, pictures of wild imagining, as well as careful copies of illustrations in story books. She had always done art, ever since she could remember, graduating from making paper dolls with cut-out clothes to entering colouring competitions in the newspaper, which she never won.

Her hunger to make pictures had been fuelled by visits to the Walker Art Gallery in Liverpool with Mum, before the war started. There were wonderful paintings in there that told a story, like the one from the Bible in which the treacherous and beautiful Delilah betrays Samson to the Philistines. And the one called "And When Did You Last See Your Father?" in which a brave little boy from a Royalist family is questioned by a stern Puritan inquisitor while his sister, guarded by a soldier, is in tears. You knew this was happening in the middle of the English Civil War and that the boy's father was on the run, possibly even hiding in that very house. There were other good paintings, too.

Joan missed the visits terribly, but they were out of the question now, because of the war. She had to make do with old sepia postcard reproductions, some of which she had pinned up on the attic wall to inspire her. The picture of her own that she was trying to get right was one of Beauty and the Beast. She kept at it for most of the afternoon, working on the Beast's face, which was the most interesting part. She was doing his eyes peering out from a great hairy mane and a huge jaw with jutting teeth, but she wanted to make him look a bit sad too, because he was really a prince.

As always when she was painting, Joan lost all track of time and only when the light began to fade did she realize that it must be about half past four. Hastily, she picked up her things, carefully washed her brushes, and nipped back down the ladder.

The Russell family – Doreen, her older brother, David, and their mother and father – lived quite near by but in a much more desirable house in the very best part of town. It had big wrought-iron gates, a sweeping half-circle of gravel drive, and a lot of mock-Tudor gables.

There was a separate double garage with a shiny car in it, which, unlike almost everyone else's, was not laid up for the duration of the war but very much in use. This was because Mr Russell was doing a very important job with the Mersey Docks and Harbour Board, organizing vital supplies of food and armaments that merchant ships brought into the Liverpool docks.

The back of the house offered a wide view of the estuary, with huge skies and silvery rippling mud.

By now the coast of North Wales was fading to a dark shape and hardly visible. No lights showed from the house, of course, because of the strict blackout rules, but when Doreen answered the door and led Joan into their big front room – the lounge, they called it – it was warm and welcoming.

Mr and Mrs Russell were sitting by the fire on a big leather settee. There was a grand piano with music on it, already lit by a standard lamp, and lots of bookcases. David was balanced against the back of an armchair, reading the paper. He put it down when he saw Joan and gave her a big friendly grin. Mrs Russell sprang welcomingly to her feet.

Unlike Ross and Derek, David did not seem to suffer from spots. His skin was the smooth olive kind, and his hair had a bit of an auburn glint to it. He was fifteen, the same age as Brian, but he was in the scholarship class at the grammar school because he was hoping to get into Cambridge. Joan often saw him on his bicycle, pedalling purposefully to and from school, and he always waved. But meeting him like this in his own home was, just for a moment, a little overwhelming. She quickly turned towards Mrs Russell's inviting smile and outstretched hand.

"Joan! How lovely to see you! How are your mother and the rest of the family?"

"We're OK, thanks."

"I'm dying to hear all the news. I hardly seem to get time for anything now that I'm driving this lorry for the WVS. They keep one at it till all hours! But won't you have something to eat before the cinema?"

"No, thank you," said Joan. She would have loved to have said, "Yes, please," because she was very hungry, but in this era of food rationing, it wasn't polite to accept food. Mrs Russell picked up a plate of biscuits from the coffee table.

"Do have one of these at least. We've just had a food parcel from America – a lucky windfall!"

"They're delicious!" added Doreen, munching greedily.

Joan relaxed and took one.

Mrs Russell was not at all like the mothers of her other school friends. Most of them were kind enough, but tended to be wearily overburdened by war work and food rationing. They huddled in shapeless cardigans and tied their hair up in headscarves. Mrs Russell's hair was short, ruffled and untidy, but it was the same lovely honey colour as Doreen's.

She was wearing slacks and an old open-neck shirt which she managed to make look like something out of a sportswear ad in *Vogue* magazine. One of the nicest things about her, though, was that she always seemed to have time to chat.

"I expect you and your mother will be going to this charity dinner dance at the golf club?" she said. "I'm on the organizing committee, worse luck. Captain Harper Jones roped me into it. I can't think why. I only hope the air-raid siren doesn't start up as soon as we've got things going."

Doreen pulled a face. "Do we *have* to go? It is likely to be pretty awful. He'll have no idea how to get hold of a proper band. It'll be all old married people doing waltzes and foxtrots."

"Oh, he's not such a bad fellow," said her father. "I work with him quite a lot at the docks and he's very efficient. Anything he organizes is bound to go like clockwork, I should think."

"Well, I'll only come if you'll promise not to dance with him, Mummy. He looks so silly when he's trying to smooch around on the dance floor, sticking out his fat behind."

Joan said nothing. She quickly glanced at David,

but he had carefully detached himself from the conversation by returning to his newspaper. She was hot with embarrassment at the thought of her own mum dancing in public with Captain Harper Jones. Even worse was the thought of David being there to witness it. Happily, Mr Russell changed the subject.

"Doreen tells me how good you are at art, Joan," he said. "How I envy you. If there's one thing I wish I could do more than any other, it's being able to draw."

"Her homework exercise books are full of amazing drawings all over the margins," said Doreen. "They are absolutely wizard!"

"Is there any particular painter you admire?" Mr Russell asked.

"Well, Mum and I used to go to the Walker Art Gallery in Liverpool before the war started..." Joan trailed off, shy but pleased by the compliments.

"What a shame that it's no longer possible to go and see the paintings. But I've got a whole collection of art books here that you're welcome to borrow any time. Lots of stuff on the Impressionists and more modern painters too, if you're interested. Have a look next time you come to see us."

"Thanks. I'd really like to!"

"Hey – we've got to go!" said Doreen, jumping up. "We'll miss the Pathé news and the trailer before the main feature if we don't hurry."

CHAPTER 7

The Queensway Cinema was near the promenade – a draughty one-storey building lurking behind a shabby Art Deco façade. There was no smartly uniformed commissionaire standing outside to marshal the queue as there was at the big Odeon cinema in Liverpool; just a placard outside telling you what was showing and the prices of seats, which was difficult to read in the blackout. The lady who sold the tickets sat inside in her glass-fronted box office wearing a scarf and overcoat. A few servicemen from the nearby Royal Air Force station and their girlfriends were drifting in, and a gaggle of sixth formers from the secondary school. Most of the older crowd, like Audrey and Dai, were at the local hop down at the church hall.

A bored girl in an usherette uniform shone her torch to guide Joan and Doreen into their seats somewhere in the middle of the auditorium. The back rows were unofficially reserved for couples. They had double seats – "cosies" – with the arms between them removed to facilitate the complicated manoeuvre of cuddling up to somebody when the lights were low. Before the lights were lowered, it was possible for the rest of the audience to have an up-to-the-minute take on who was dating who. As soon as they were seated, Doreen miraculously produced a packet of crisps (another windfall from the American food parcel) and the two friends munched happily as they settled down to the show.

First there were the ads, which Joan found a bit dull. Shakily projected onto an elaborately draped curtain that masked the screen, they were mostly for local shops and cafes:

"Beat the Blitz at Handley's Hardware Store! High-quality ironmongery at pre-war prices. Blackout shades always in stock."

"Knit for victory! Wool, fancy goods and haberdashery. Unbeatable quality at Madame Beazley's!"

"Jack's Bicycle Shop! Repairs, and bikes for sale and hire."

"The OK Cafe, two doors down from this cinema. Open till seven p.m."

After the ads, the curtains parted and the Pathé newsreel began. Accompanied by a relentlessly optimistic commentary, it showed pictures of King George VI and Queen Elizabeth inspecting bomb damage in the East End of London, followed by cheerful British troops on the march, then women hard at work in munitions factories and something about the Italian invasion of Greece. Finally, there was a clip from a stirring speech given in Washington by the President of the United States, the recently re-elected and hugely popular Franklin D. Roosevelt.

The trailer for next week's film followed. It was *The Philadelphia Story*, starring Katharine Hepburn and Cary Grant.

"I'm definitely coming to see this," whispered Doreen. "Cary's just *so* glamorous."

"Jimmy Stewart's in it too," said Joan. "I think I like him better!"

At last the main film started. But they were not long into it, with Betty Grable dancing and singing her way through the first big number, when they heard the heart-sinking wail of the air-raid siren outside.

"Oh, Lord!" said Joan. "I've never known a raid start as early as this. It's only been dark for about an hour. My mum'll be going off the deep end."

The film stopped abruptly, the house lights went up, and the cinema manager stood in front of the screen and told everyone to keep calm, advising them to stay under cover until the all clear sounded. The show would be resumed shortly.

"My parents will have gone out by now," said Doreen. "They were going over to see some friends – walking, of course. Daddy never uses the car except for his war work. He says it's unpatriotic, so I expect they'll have to stay under cover like us."

Betty Grable soon reappeared on the screen and the audience settled down, uneasily. Everyone was listening out for any kind of noise. For quite a while there was silence outside – an unusual stillness. Then they heard it, quite clearly above the film soundtrack: the throb of aircraft engines, far away at first, but getting steadily louder.

"Heading for Liverpool..." muttered the man in the row behind them.

Joan couldn't concentrate on the film. Her ears, like everyone else's, were straining to catch the sound of those engines getting nearer: German Focke-Wulf bombers on their way to drop their nightly barrage of high explosives to pound the Liverpool docks.

Joan glanced fearfully up at the ceiling of the cinema. It did not look particularly solid to her. There was a kind of ramshackle glass skylight in the middle, with makeshift blinds, that looked as though it might give way at the slightest impact, let alone a direct hit. She could not help wondering if the cinema manager's instruction to stay under cover was such good advice after all. Those German aircraft would not be aiming at their suburban area, she knew that, but, flying at night, they had been known to make mistakes.

The raid lasted about three and a half hours, by which time they had seen both *Down Argentine Way* and the newsreel played twice. Every so often the electricity went off, and they were plunged into darkness. It was terrifying when this happened, and Joan was so relieved when the picture reappeared on the screen, somewhat jerkily. Nobody in the audience panicked – one girl in the back row was crying and clinging to her boyfriend, but most people remained grimly silent. They all knew that to make for the exits at this point would be more dangerous than sitting tight. The air was dense with cigarette smoke.

They could hear the distant sickening crunch and thud of explosions over Liverpool and the accompanying cracks of anti-aircraft gunfire. Once or twice the ceiling shook badly, and flakes of plaster floated down like grubby snowflakes onto their heads.

Doreen was amazingly brave. Every time there was a particularly frightening noise, her hand tightened on Joan's arm, but she kept looking resolutely at the screen. Joan did likewise, determined to match her courage.

When at last the all clear sounded, the whole audience scrambled to their feet, struggling into their overcoats as they crowded towards the exits. Joan and Doreen were caught up in the rush. Outside, they joined other strangers in shaking hands and wishing one another good luck and a safe journey home. It was a starless night, but the sky over Liverpool was blazing orange and fiery red.

"The fire and ambulance services'll be busy over there tonight," said one man. His wife only shivered.

Neither Joan nor Doreen had remembered to bring their little electric torches. They set off silently, arm in arm, into the blacked-out street. It was not yet nine o'clock, but they were so tired they could hardly walk. A hurrying figure loomed out of the darkness ahead of them and a powerful flashlight was shone into their faces. It was David.

"Doreen! Joan! Are you OK? Everybody was out except me, so I thought I'd better come and meet you."

Doreen threw her arms around him. "Oh, Dave! We were in there for *ages*. They showed the film over and over. We thought the roof was going to fall in on us all!"

"I'm not surprised. It's probably held together with Sellotape."

He took them both by the arm, and the three of them walked on together. When they reached the Russells' house and David had seen Doreen safely inside, he turned to Joan and said, "It's pretty late. I'd better take you home."

"No, I'll be all right, really."

"Come on."

They walked in silence. Normal chit-chat was out

of the question at this point, and anyway Joan could not think of anything to say. The evening had been overwhelming. When they reached her front gate and she turned to thank him, they were interrupted by Mum's frantic appearance on the doorstep.

"Joan! Is that you? Thank heavens! I've been worried stiff about you. Brian's staying with a friend, and Audrey and Dai are at the dance, so I couldn't leave Judy on her own in the middle of an air raid and—"

"It's OK, Mum," Joan said wearily. "We had to stay under cover until the all clear went, and then David came to meet us." She was so glad to be home.

"Oh – it's *David*! How kind of you to bring Joan home. Won't you come in?"

"No, thanks, Mrs Armitage. I'd better be getting back."

"Well, if you're sure. Thank you so much."

"Yes, thanks a lot," Joan said.

She stood for a moment, watching the light of his torch bob away up the road, then walked slowly into the house.

CHAPTER 8

As the autumn wore on and the days grew shorter, a storm cloud loomed heavily on Joan's horizon: the golf club dinner dance. The thought of having to get through a dinner with Mum and Captain Harper Jones, then sit there watching them dancing – perhaps even (heaven forbid!) cheek to cheek – was depressing. Worse, Doreen and her family, and maybe even David, would be there to witness it. But Joan's efforts to get out of it were in vain. Excuses like having nothing to wear were briskly brushed aside by Mum.

"You can wear Audrey's blue velvet dress, and I'll lend you my diamanté clip," she said.

"I'd look silly in that frock. Everyone'll know it's not mine. They've seen Audrey wearing it."

"Of course they won't. People don't remember things like that."

"But I haven't got any decent shoes. And don't suggest I borrow Audrey's, because my feet are much bigger than hers."

"Don't worry. You can wear your best black patent leather ones. You'll look lovely. And there'll be some really good food. Ronnie's managing to lay on an excellent three-course meal. I don't know how he does it in these difficult times."

Joan said nothing. She knew it was useless to resist.

The big room at the golf club, which was usually the bar area, had been cleared to make room for dancing. A live band – piano, drums, saxophone and clarinet – was setting up in one corner when Joan and Mum arrived. Captain Ronnie Harper Jones had been there most of the day, setting up dining tables in the adjoining room and checking that the blackout shutters were in place. A large vanload of food had arrived from Liverpool and had been unpacked and laid out on the buffet table. It was an excellent spread, as promised: a rare treat in wartime. But Joan was dreading the dancing that followed too much to relish the sight.

She looked anxiously about to see if anyone her own age had arrived yet. Ross and Derek were nowhere to be seen, of course. Their families were probably not invited, even if they could afford to come. This was strictly an officer-class event. She spotted a few girls from school, although mercifully not Angela Travis. Gradually the room filled with guests. They were mostly, as Doreen had predicted, middle-aged people, but some had a few uneasy teenagers in tow. Drinks were served and the older people made bright conversation.

This is going to be even worse than I expected, thought Joan. But when the Russell family walked in, the atmosphere lightened up considerably. Doreen and her mother led the way, looking lovely. Mr Russell and David strode behind. Joan had never seen David wearing a suit before. Ronnie Harper Jones rushed over and greeted them enthusiastically. He even kissed Mrs Russell's hand, then fell into a long conversation with Mr Russell. The rest of the family came straight over to where Joan and her mother were sitting.

"Oh, I'm so glad you made it," Mrs Russell said, giving Mum a kiss. "And you too, Joan. You're both looking marvellous. We're going to need all the moral support we can get when the dancing begins."

Doreen shot Joan a quick glance and rolled her eyes. David said nothing.

Sadly, the two families were not seated anywhere near each other during dinner. Joan was trapped next to Ronnie, with Mum on his other side. She was too oppressed by the sound of his braying voice ringing out across the table to do more than toy with her food. Then the moment she'd dreaded arrived. The band struck up with their first number, a current hit called "You Are My Sunshine", and people started to move towards the dance floor.

Ronnie and Mum were among the first, and he lost no time in showing off his nifty footwork. Ignoring the plodding "slow, slow, quick, quick, slow", which most couples of his age were happy to settle for, he went straight into some complex double-reverse turns. He even tried swinging Mum around with one hand while (as Doreen had also so accurately predicted) sticking out his backside.

Joan watched with a sinking heart. She wondered how long this evening was going to last. Doreen was on the dance floor too, partnered by a boy who Joan vaguely recognized as being in the same class as Brian at school.

Joan was staring down at her plate, crumbling the remains of a bread roll, when David ambled across the room and sprawled down on the chair beside her.

"Sorry I can't ask you to dance," he said. "I'm no good at it, I'm afraid. Your feet would probably never recover."

Joan smiled. "That's OK. It's rather a relief, as a matter of fact."

David helped himself to one of the delicious biscuits that had been served with the coffee.

"How's art going these days?"

"Well, OK, I guess."

"I envy you. I can't draw for toffee. And now, at school, there never seems to be time for anything but sport and the main exam subjects. I still play the piano, though, when I can."

"Classical pieces?"

"Yes, sometimes. But what I really like is playing boogie-woogie. It drives my mum mad. She doesn't much care for my jazz records either."

"Jazz? You mean dance music? Glenn Miller and Artie Shaw?"

"Well, not really. I love Louis Armstrong – he's the best trumpet player in the world! – but I like the small groups, with terrific instrumental players like Buck Clayton and Lester Young, people like that. And blues singers… Billie Holiday beats them all."

"I don't think I've ever heard of her. Is she on the radio?"

"Sometimes. But they're all black American musicians, of course."

"Oh yes, of course!" Joan said. She was trying to remember if she'd seen pictures of any of these people in Audrey's fan magazines, and vowed to find out more about them. There was a pause, in which they sat watching the dancers. Joan wanted very much to talk to David about what she really cared about, which was drawing, and her plans to try to get into art school as soon as she could, rather than stay on in the sixth form at school. But somehow she didn't feel this was an appropriate moment.

At last Doreen extricated herself from her partner and came over to join them, flopping down in a chair in mock exhaustion. "I wonder how long this will go on for," she said. "I don't know how all these oldies find the energy."

David looked at his watch. "It'll be quite a long time yet," he said grimly.

"Let's hope there isn't an air raid tonight or we'll get stuck here for hours and hours!" Joan said.

But there was no air raid that night. And when finally the band played the last waltz – "Who's Taking You Home Tonight?" – followed by "Goodnight, Sweetheart", Joan prayed that David and Doreen didn't notice Mum and Ronnie dancing cheek to cheek.

In the end, to Joan's great relief, it was only she and Mum who walked home together, side by side in the blackout, because Ronnie had to stay on to supervise the clearing up.

"I wonder what happened to all that leftover food?" said Joan.

"Oh, I expect Ronnie will see that it's given away to someone who needs it," said Mum. Then she took Joan's arm. "You didn't enjoy it much, did you, Joanie?"

"Not much. Did you?"

"Oh, yes – well, I suppose I did. Anyway, thanks for coming along."

"That's all right," said Joan. "As long as I don't ever have to do it again!"

CHAPTER 9

The Luftwaffe made up for their one night's absence with a particularly heavy raid on Liverpool the following evening. It began early, just after dark. All the family were in the back room eating supper and enjoying *Forces Favourites* on the radio when the sirens started.

Mum switched off the programme and they sat there in silence, listening. After a while they heard it, that chillingly ominous sound that was becoming all too familiar to them now – the steadily increasing drone of approaching enemy aircraft: German bombers, headed for Liverpool.

"It's too late to get down to the pubic shelter now," said Mum, doing her best to sound calm, like those people in the propaganda films with titles like *Britain Can Take It!* But her voice was a bit shaky and Joan could tell she was scared.

Mum turned off the lights, went over to the window, and peered out through a crack in the blackout blind. The rest of the family crowded behind her. They could see the searchlights springing to life and raking the sky over the city. Then the ack-ack barrage from the anti-aircraft guns began in earnest. There were sudden flashes of hectic white light from the flares that the enemy bombers were dropping to guide them to their main target, the Liverpool and Birkenhead docks.

Brian was keen to go outside and watch, but Mum shouted at him to stay where he was.

"You'd all better get under the stairs," she said. This was supposed to be the safest place to be if the house got a direct hit. But there wasn't really room for all four of them in there. Audrey refused point blank, saying she would rather go to bed. Judy, who was getting used to raids and often managed to sleep right through them, clung to Mum and started to cry.

In the end, Mum settled for getting the children into sleeping bags under the dining-room table while she sat up in an armchair, huddled in an overcoat. Joan wasn't in the least bit sleepy. Sleep was totally impossible under these circumstances. She just lay there, trying to avoid Judy's knees sticking into her back and listening to her miserable grizzling. They could hear the barrage steadily intensify, the guns on the high ground above Liverpool and Birkenhead keeping up a constant fire.

The crazy thing is, I just can't believe that any of us are going to be killed, Joan thought to herself. But she knew very well that, although their suburb was supposed to be a relatively safe area with no military objectives, the German bombers often dropped their unused bombs at random on their way home, to lighten their load.

The raid seemed to go on endlessly. It was well after midnight when at last the all clear sounded. Judy had long since fallen into a deep sleep, and had to be scooped up and carried to bed by Mum. Audrey, yawning and stretching her cramped back and legs, followed. Joan and Brian were still wide awake. They hovered on the landing, and Brian, careful not to show a light, peered out of the window. The searchlights were gone now, leaving the sky over

Liverpool a fierce, sullen red, heavy with smoke and reflecting flames from the burning docks.

"They must have dropped a lot of incendiary bombs," said Brian.

"I'm glad it wasn't on us," Joan said, then stopped short, realizing what a heartless remark that was when so many people's homes must have been destroyed. Heartless too, she thought, that even though she knew that people had died in those fires, the sight of them lighting up the sky seemed unreal somehow, like those paintings she had seen of infernos and shipwrecks at sea and visions of hell. But it would have been only too real if *their* home had taken a direct hit. Joan shivered.

Their little back garden and the golf links lay shrouded in darkness. It was high tide. All they could hear now was the sound of waves washing in peacefully beyond the sand dunes.

"Come on, you two," Mum called out wearily. "Time you were in bed."

Brian trudged off to his room, but Joan hesitated for one last look. Just before she turned away, she thought she caught sight of a movement near the fence – something like the figure of a man standing under the pear tree. But, when she looked again, he was gone.

CHAPTER 10

It was the morning after the raid and a Saturday. As Joan had a day off from youth service, Mum asked her to queue at Barrett's the butcher's. It was always a long queue, especially if word had got round that there was a chance of some sausages, or maybe even lamb chops, so she set out early. It was a chore she hated, but it made a change from collecting scrap metal. The queue was mostly made up of women, looking tired out, with headscarves tied turban-like over curlers. They were all talking about last night's air raid.

"They say Huyton and Childwall got it last night, as well as the docks," one woman said. "My auntie lives over there. I'm dead worried about her.

I couldn't get through to her on the phone. They've been dropping landmines – those awful things, floating down on parachutes."

"My hubby was on roof-spotting duty all night with the ARP," said another. "I was right glad to see him back this morning, I can tell you."

A third chipped in, "Mine's an air-raid warden. It drives me mad that they always expect him to turn up for work at the factory first thing next morning, even though he's been up all night and is dead on his feet."

They lapsed into a gloomy silence. Joan was dreading her turn to face Mr Barrett. He was a large man with a bristling moustache, waxed at the ends, and great hands, mottled purplish red, the colour of the raw meat he attacked with such vigour on his chopping board. Once, for a dare, Joan and Brian had telephoned him anonymously and enquired if he had pigs' trotters. When he said yes, they giggled and came back with, "Hard luck! What are you going to do about it, then?" and rang off. Hilarious though it had been at the time, she'd always had an uneasy feeling that he knew they were the culprits.

"Chops are off," he said, eyeing her coldly when it came to her turn. "I can let you have a bit of liver."

"Oh, yes – thanks," said Joan meekly, and watched as he expertly sliced up a rather meagre portion of meat with his big knife and slapped it onto a sheet of newspaper. Joan paid Mrs Barrett, his thin, exhausted-looking wife, who sat clipping out ration coupons at the cash till, then hurried outside.

The first person she ran into was Doreen, also armed with a shopping basket, her hair blowing all over her face. It was a sight that cheered Joan up enormously.

"Let's go for a coffee at the Bluebell," said Doreen, linking arms. "It might give us a bit of energy for the next queue."

On the way there, they saw Ania with Miss Mellor. She was walking two steps behind her hostess, eyes down, carrying the shopping basket. The two of them looked as though they were all set for a long queue at the grocer's. No chance of a morning coffee for her.

"Poor Ania," Doreen said. "She always seems so lonely. Can you imagine leaving your whole family behind to move somewhere you don't know anyone?"

The Bluebell Cafe was where all the upper-class ladies of the district gathered on Saturday mornings to exchange gossip. Joan's mum never went there.

She regarded most of them as a lot of time-wasting snobs. But it was warm inside, and if you got a seat by the window, you could watch the world go by.

"Wasn't the dance *awful*?" said Doreen, when they were settled. "Mum and Dad had to *force* David to go. He hates dancing. He says he's scared of treading on some poor girl's toes."

"I don't blame him! Mum had to force me too."

"As for Captain Harper Jones!" Doreen rolled her eyes. "Thank heavens we were spared the sight of him doing the tango."

Joan felt uncomfortable. The sight of him dancing with Mum was still raw in her memory.

"My dad quite likes him," Doreen went on. "They play golf together sometimes, and he says he's quite a good chap when you get to know him. And he certainly knows how to lay on a good dinner."

Joan quickly changed the subject.

When Joan arrived home, the liver was already dripping blood through the newspaper. Surprisingly, Mum was still sitting at the breakfast table among the unwashed dishes. Joan usually took Mum's appearance for granted unless she had done something radical like change her hairstyle, but she could not help noticing how strained and tired she looked.

Brian had gone off to do his youth-service training as a bicycle messenger and Judy, busy cutting out paper dolls, was being quite cooperative for once. Audrey, meanwhile, could be heard talking urgently on the telephone in the hall. When she put the receiver down and walked into the kitchen, there were tears streaming down her cheeks.

She had been talking to Dai. His ship had docked at Liverpool yesterday, just before the Blitz began, but all shore leave had been cancelled because of damage from last night's raid. As always, security was very strict and he was not allowed to say anything about how long they were likely to be in port. All he could tell her was that as soon as the dock was clear enough to start reloading, they would probably prepare to re-embark immediately.

"The phone line got cut off before we had any time to talk properly," Audrey sobbed. "It's so awful him not getting any shore leave – at all! And heaven knows how long he'll be away on the next trip. It'll be to America probably. And I can't help thinking about all those Nazi U-boats out there.

On the news they try to play down the losses, but we're losing merchant ships all the time. And they haven't even got the depth charges and guns to fight back, like they have on Royal Navy destroyers—" She stopped abruptly, falling silent. Normally, it was a kind of unwritten rule in their family not to talk about their anxieties like this. Mum always did her level best to keep everyone's spirits up by turning the conversation to something more hopeful. Today she looked too exhausted to try. She just sat there, slumped in her chair.

It was then that Joan noticed her flushed face.

"Are you OK, Mum?" she asked.

"Yes, yes, of course. Just a bit tired, that's all."

"But you're burning hot!"

Mum, who was never ever ill, who kept going with such accustomed regularity that none of them could remember when she had last allowed herself even a modest late morning in bed, was clearly running a temperature.

"Better take some aspirin," Joan suggested anxiously.

"There's some in the bathroom cupboard. I'll get them," Mum said. She tried to stand but fell back again onto her chair and for a moment looked as though she was going to faint.

"Mum, Mum, what's the matter, Mum?" squeaked Judy.

"Oh, shut up, Judy!" snapped Audrey. After wiping away her tears with the back of her hand, she said, much more gently, "Come on, Mum – better lie down for a bit."

Mum put up no resistance as they helped her over to the sofa, where she lay back and closed her eyes. Joan ran to fetch a blanket and mix two aspirins in a glass of water.

"I'll be all right in a minute," said Mum weakly. "I think I might have caught the flu. There's so much of it around at the moment. I was with someone the other day who had it. I'll just rest here for a bit, if you'll clear the table. I must go into town this afternoon."

"Town" to them meant Birkenhead or Liverpool rather than their local suburban high street.

"Don't be daft, Mum," said Audrey. "You can't go anywhere at the moment except to bed."

"But I must go!" Mum protested. "I promised to collect a whole lot of stuff – bandages and dressings and things – for the Red Cross emergency first-aid centre. They rang this morning to say that they're running very low on supplies. Nothing's been getting through from the main depot in Birkenhead because of the Blitz. The local ambulance broke down in last night's raid, and they haven't been able to get a replacement yet – so I promised to go over by train to fetch them. They're depending on me."

"*Definitely* not, Mum," said Audrey firmly. "Look, why can't Joan and I go? We can manage it easily together. I know where the depot is – quite near the station. We can drop Judy off at the Hemmings' house on our way to catch the train and be back long before teatime."

Mum hesitated – and then took a deep breath and lay back, too worn out to disagree.

"All right," she said. "If you really think you can manage it before it gets dark. There may be another raid tonight and you must be back before then."

"There's plenty of time. We can easily do it if we get going right now. Come on, Joan, Judy, get your coats."

CHAPTER 11

It was not until they had dropped Judy off and reached the station that it dawned on Joan just how excited Audrey was at the prospect of this trip. She had even managed a lightning change into her best suit and a clean white blouse, and her recently tear-stained face was now meticulously made up. The train was just drawing in as they ran up to the ticket office. Audrey plonked down the money and asked for two returns to Liverpool. Joan was surprised, but there was no time to ask why as Audrey hurried her over the bridge to the platform. They jumped on the train just as the doors were closing.

"Why did you get tickets to Liverpool?" asked Joan as soon as they were settled on board. "I thought we were only going as far as Birkenhead."

"We are. But we're going on to Liverpool after that."

"*What?* Whatever for?"

Audrey looked out at the suburban back gardens racing past the train window.

"I'm going to try to get to the docks, of course," she said. "I've got a pretty good idea of where Dai's ship will be. It was in the Gladstone Dock last time, so I'm guessing it will be there again."

"*Audrey!* You're not going to try to meet Dai?"

"Why not? Even if I only get as far as the dock's entrance, I might be able to get a message to him to come and meet me."

"You're *crazy!*"

"Oh, Joanie, don't be cross. I've just *got* to see Dai, even if it's only for a few minutes. And I needed you to help me. Mum would never have let me go on my own, so this errand to get the Red Cross stuff came in really handy. We can easily make it home before it gets dark."

"You mean to tell me that we are going to collect all these packages then lug them all the way to the Liverpool docks and back?"

"They won't be very heavy – they're only bandages, cotton wool and stuff. And you won't have to come all the way to the docks with me. I can leave you somewhere and we can meet up afterwards."

Joan knew there was no stopping Audrey once she had made up her mind to do something. They sat in silence for the rest of the journey.

The Red Cross depot at Birkenhead was not far from the station. They hurried over there and managed to make it back, carrying the packages, in good time to catch the next train on to Liverpool Central.

When they emerged into the crowded street, the first thing they saw were the windows of a department store that had been blown out in a blast from last night's Blitz. Shattered glass lay all over the pavement, waiting to be swept away. Workmen were busy putting up temporary shutters over the gaping, ruined window displays, where a few bedraggled fashion dummies remained exposed, looking anything but elegant.

People were picking their way through the rubble. Servicemen and servicewomen of many different nationalities mingled with harassed civilians who were shouldering their way through the crowd, anxious to get some shopping done before the next night's raid began. Joan felt sick. The sight of those ruined shops really brought home the danger of being in Liverpool.

Audrey immediately took control. She lead the way purposefully towards Lime Street, with Joan trailing reluctantly behind her. But, as always, there was a certain buzz, a rush of adrenalin, from being engulfed by this city, even in its current battered and chaotic state. For them it still held memories of thrilling shopping expeditions with Mum before the war started or of setting out on those breathlessly anticipated visits to the Christmas pantomime at the Empire Theatre, which starred George Formby with his ukulele, followed by a cream tea with delectable cakes at the Kardomah Cafe.

The theatres and cinemas were still valiantly keeping going in spite of the Blitz, and with so many servicemen in town, the dance halls were packed too, especially on Saturday nights. Audrey sometimes went to one of the halls with Dai when he was on leave. But Mum would never think of allowing Joan anywhere near one. She said Joan was much too young to go into Liverpool in the evenings, even with a girlfriend. Mum rarely came herself now, except in the daytime to do some essential shopping. Joan didn't care tuppence about not being able to go to dance halls. It was visits to the theatre and the Walker Art Gallery that she missed most. Now she just had to make do with the local cinema.

She followed Audrey as they made their way towards the dock area, juggling their parcels. It was a fairly long walk. The big crowds thinned out slightly when they left the main shopping streets behind, but there were still plenty of people around: men loitering outside pubs, women pushing old prams loaded with babies and shopping, and children everywhere, shouting and playing in rubble-strewn side streets. Traffic was heavy in the main thoroughfare, with big lorries, already on the move again after last night's raid, making their way to and from the docks.

Audrey stopped on a long, narrow street lined with warehouses. "Can you wait for me here?" she asked. "I won't be long, I promise."

"But why?" Joan asked, dismayed. "Why can't I come with you?"

"Because I want to go on my own," said Audrey. "We're pretty near to the dock entrance now. If I can get to see Dai, even if it's only for a few minutes, we need to be alone, see? Anyway, we've carried these wretched bags quite far enough. You wait here with them. I'll be back quite soon, honest."

Joan looked around anxiously. "I don't like it," she said. "Us getting separated, I mean. Mum would have a fit if she knew about this."

But Audrey wasn't listening. She was already checking her hair and make-up in her handbag mirror. Then she briefly flung an arm around Joan's shoulders.

"I'm sorry to do this to you, Joanie," she said, "but it's just *so* important to me. You do understand, don't you?"

Before Joan could answer, Audrey was off down the street, her high heels skidding rather unsteadily on the cobbles.

Now all Joan could do was wait. She knew from experience that Audrey's vague promise of not being long was totally unreliable. She only wished that she hadn't been dumped quite so near to a corner pub from which a raucous noise emanated. It was meant to be pub closing hours, but a group of heavily made-up girls who looked not much older than Audrey were chatting and laughing with some sailors just outside the doors. Joan felt self-conscious. *It's too late to move now,* she thought. There was nothing for it but to stay put.

She looked at her watch. It was nearly four o'clock – not long before it would get dark. With a heavy sigh, she sat down on one of the bundles – she was beyond caring about squashing the contents now, however important they might be to the war effort – and watched the lorries trundling past.

Miss Sanderson had told Joan's class at school that many of these long-distance vehicles were driven by intrepid Auxiliary Territorial Service drivers, who worked in teams of two, taking it in turns to drive while the other slept in the back. They were setting out from port to deliver the strictly rationed food, which had come in at such risk to the merchant ships, all over the country to be fairly distributed among a hungry British population.

"They're a vital lifeline," Miss Sanderson had said. "We all need to dig for victory here, by growing as many carrots, cabbages and potatoes in our back gardens and allotments as we can. But there's no way we can survive without imports from abroad, and the crews aboard merchant ships are risking their lives to bring them to us – so we must waste nothing."

Joan, who could hardly remember what a banana tasted like, found herself thinking about Dai and his fellow merchant seamen as she watched the traffic go by. Among the army vehicles and big commercial trucks with suppliers' names emblazoned on the sides were smaller local lorries. They all made slow progress, stopping and starting, as they queued to get away from the dock area and begin their proper journey. Joan gazed at them as they passed. She was tired out. It seemed like a very long time since breakfast and she longed to get this awful trip over and go home. She knew Mum would be terribly anxious if they returned late, and that would be extra bad for her, as she was feeling ill.

Now the long line of lorries and vans slowed and came to a standstill right in front of her. One of them, a medium-sized unmarked vehicle – not an army one – was idling its engine a few feet away from where she was sitting. There were two men in the front. She couldn't see the driver, but the other one was leaning his elbow on the open window nearest to her, drumming his fingers and looking impatiently at the way ahead. If he had glanced down, their eyes would have met. It was fortunate that they didn't, because Joan recognized him at once, even though he wasn't in uniform.

It was Captain Ronnie Harper Jones.

CHAPTER 12

For a second Joan thought of calling out to him. She had the crazy idea that he might even offer Audrey and her a lift home in the back of the van. But she immediately thought better of it, especially as Audrey was nowhere to be seen and there was no knowing when she would turn up again. Anyway, it was already too late. The traffic jam had eased and the whole column began to move forward.

Joan settled down again with her chin on her hands. She thought gloomily that she seemed fated to keep encountering Ronnie all over the place. Exactly what he was doing here she had no idea. She imagined it was something to do with his work with the Army Catering Corps. At least it was better than seeing him at their house. If only Mum wouldn't encourage him! Surely she couldn't *like* him, not all that much? Not enough to want to dance cheek to cheek with him? But clearly she did.

Again, Joan checked her watch. She wished she had something to read or, better still, that she had her sketchbook with her. She could have done some drawing to pass the time. But she didn't even have a newspaper, let alone a pencil and paper.

It was an enormous relief to see Audrey running back up the street at last. But she was crying again. Her ruined make-up was blotched all over her cheeks. Joan put a comforting arm around her.

"Did you see Dai?" she asked.

Audrey shook her head and, for a while, she was mute with unhappiness. Then she said, "They wouldn't let me anywhere near the dock. There were lots of people going in and out of the entrances, but they were all dockers with passes. I told them at the gate that it was really urgent and asked them if they could get a message through, but they wouldn't listen. Told me to get off home quick sharp before it gets any darker."

"I suppose we'd better do that," said Joan. "No

use staying here now. And we've really got to get back to Mum, Audrey. She'll be worried stiff, and it won't do her any good wondering where we are when she's feeling ill."

Wearily, they picked up the bundles, which seemed heavier than before, and began the long trudge back to the station. Audrey's high heels were hurting her. This time it was Joan who led the way. They were both too despondent to speak. Once they chose a wrong turn and it took some time to get back onto the right route.

They were still making their way down the street that they hoped was the quickest way back to Liverpool Central station when the sirens started. The road they were on began to empty right away. People pushed past them, dragging children by the hand, as they made for the air-raid shelters. An Air Raid Precautions warden in a white helmet hurried up to them.

"Looks like a daylight raid," he said. "You girls had better get into the shelter with the others as quick as you can."

"But we *can't*!" said Audrey, distraught. "My sister and I are expected home. We've *got* to get to Central station."

The warden shook his head firmly.

"No, no. The trains probably won't even be running right now, anyway. You'll have to take cover till it's over." And he began to shepherd them along with the others.

Audrey dissolved into tears again, and Joan felt desperate. Everything seemed to be conspiring against them today, and being delayed by an air raid at this juncture was more than she could bear. Mum would be frantic with worry. But at that moment there came a shout from behind them.

"Just a moment, officer!"

A private car had pulled onto the kerb and a man jumped out. It was Mr Russell! He greeted Joan and Audrey briefly, and, to his eternal credit, did not waste time on asking them what on earth they were doing in this part of Liverpool. He simply addressed himself directly to the air-raid warden, showing his identity card.

"These two young ladies are neighbours of ours. I'm on my way home with my wife, who just came off an eight-hour shift as a van driver. I think they might be safer if we gave them a lift home with us, out of the danger area. I don't mind driving through this, and I've been told that the Mersey Tunnel is still open."

The harassed warden hesitated, but only for a moment. He had a great many other people to think about.

"All right, sir – it might be best if you will take full responsibility for getting them home. I'm consigning them to your care. Understand?"

Joan and Audrey, clutching their packages, had jumped in the back of the car almost before he had finished speaking.

It took some time for Mr Russell to manoeuvre a way through the traffic, but with some skilful driving, they were soon on their way. It was only then that Audrey had recovered enough to explain, with tears in her eyes, their whole disastrous errand. "They wouldn't let me near the dock," she told them. "Wouldn't let me see Dai. And he's going away again soon."

Mrs Russell listened sympathetically. She was particularly concerned about their mum being ill.

"Please don't tell her where we met," said Audrey. "I mean, that we were in Liverpool. She'd only get upset."

"Of course. I won't say a word about it if you'd rather I didn't," Mrs Russell said. "The most important thing is to get you back as soon as possible so you can look after her. This alert might be a false alarm – they often are. But there may well be another Blitz tonight and we must get you out of here before then. I tell you what, why don't you let us deliver those parcels to our local Red Cross dressing station? We can run them over in the car. Then you can get straight home."

"Oh, Mrs Russell – would you really?"

It was very dark by the time the Russells dropped the girls back at their front door. "Send your mother our love. I hope she feels better soon," Mrs Russell called after them.

Brian was in the hall. "Whatever took you so long?" he said. "Mum's asleep. I made her a hot drink, but she wouldn't eat anything. Good job she hasn't woken up or she would have started doing her nut about where you two had got to."

Joan and Audrey were both too exhausted to explain their terrible day all over again. Luckily Brian hadn't seen Mr Russell's car.

"Is Judy still at the Hemmings'?" asked Audrey, changing the subject.

"Yes," said Brian. "I rang them earlier and they've offered to have her for the night."

"Thank goodness for that," said Joan. The thought of getting Judy to bed would have been the last straw. All three of them trailed dejectedly into the back room.

"Is there anything for supper?" Brian asked. "I'm starving!"

CHAPTER 13

It took a week for Mum to fully recover from the flu and regain her usual energetic drive.

"I was wondering," she said to Joan one evening over the washing up, "about that Polish girl at your school – the one you told me about. Ania, wasn't it? It must be very dull for her, living with that old lady. Why don't you ask her over here for tea one day?"

Joan's heart sank. She felt sorry for Ania, but she didn't really want to make friends with her. Ania had settled down in the class, up to a point, and had even managed to keep her head down enough to keep clear of Angela Travis and her gang most of the time, but it was still almost impossible to get a word out of her outside the classroom. All Joan wanted to do was to let well alone.

"I could make a cake," said Mum. "I've got some icing sugar and margarine saved up and some dried egg powder. *Do* ask her. It would be a kind thing to do, surely, to offer her a bit of hospitality?"

There was no arguing with this. So after school the following Friday afternoon, Joan and Ania walked back to Joan's house together. Joan had tried to get Doreen to come too, but she had cried off.

Mum had done her very best with the tea. She had even got hold of some chocolate biscuits, an almost unheard-of luxury these days. Ania ate ravenously and thanked Joan's mum politely many times between mouthfuls. After tea, conversation stalled somewhat.

"Would you like to go for a walk while I clear up?" Mum suggested. "Or would you rather listen to a comedy show on the radio?"

Ania preferred the first suggestion. "Radio I do not like," she explained. "They talk so fast and I do not understand well the jokes."

So she and Joan set out. For some time they walked in silence, heading towards the promenade for lack of anywhere better to go. It was chilly, and there were very few people about. The tide was out, and the big bank of clouds that had built up over the faraway Welsh coastline was the same colour as the estuary mud.

"You must get awfully sick of walking around here," Joan said at last. "I mean, there's not much to do, is there?"

"I am – what is the word? – accustomed. Yes, accustomed," answered Ania, simply. "I have stayed in so many places – more that I can count. Miss Mellor, the lady I live with now, does not wish me to be at home with her in the daytime. And…" She paused and then went on, "Neither do I wish to be with her."

Ania plodded on, looking carefully at her feet. There was a long silence before she began to speak again. This time it was in a very low voice, and it was as though a floodgate had suddenly burst open inside her, and her words poured out very rapidly. "My home I remember very well. Our house, our village."

"Your village in Poland?"

"Yes. Where we live – my mother, my father and me, and my grandmother too until she die. We work very hard, we grow our food, we have a cow, we have plenty to eat. We live well until the soldiers come."

"Nazi soldiers?"

"Yes. They come in trucks. They take all the Jewish people, all families living there. Many Jewish people live in our village. The soldiers pull them out of their houses, and line them up in the street. We are Christian Polish people, not Jewish. But my father try to help our Jewish neighbours, the Wartskis. He hide them and their children in our barn at back of house. The soldiers search the barn and they find them." She hesitated, then said, "So they take them, and my father also. Put him in truck with the others. Then they shoot our dog. Shoot him in the street because he bark and try to follow my father. Then my mother and I run away. We run out of house at back, across the field, into forest. The soldiers come after us, but we hide. Soon they stop looking and go away."

Joan took a deep breath. She couldn't think how to respond to this sudden, devastating revelation.

"Did you go back?" she asked finally.

"Yes," said Ania. "We arc too frightened at first. So we wait until dark, then we go back. We find the truck quite gone. The truck taking my father. Gone. We do not know where. We find our village – what is the word? – all spoiled, all broken, many houses burned. Our house still there, but all our things smashed. My mother and I know we cannot stay there. We fear too much that the soldiers will come back. So Mother look and find the box that my father hide under the floor, next to fireplace. Still there. The box with the money he save, and my grandmother's gold chain and her ring. My mother, she put them in a little bag around her neck. Then we put on warm clothes and take what we can carry and leave our home. And we start to walk."

Joan and Ania had come to a standstill, leaning on the railings and looking out towards a final burst of blood-red sun dropping down below the Welsh coastline.

"Where did you go?" asked Joan.

Ania said, "We walk for many days. I do not know how far we walk. My mother say we must get to her brother's house. There we will be safe. There are many other people on the road like us. Some have carts. Sometimes they let us ride, but not often, because they too have all their things, and children also. So we walk until we reach the railway station. Many, many people there. When the train come, we must push and fight to get on. We journey on the train many hours. We have little food and no water. If the train stop, we get off and run to fill our water bottles at the tap by side of track. One girl in our truck, she get out to … to…" She blushed.

"To relieve herself?"

Ania nodded. "But the train move on and we must leave her there. Her father and mother scream, try to stop the train. But they cannot. The girl is lost, left there by the railway."

"Did you reach your uncle?"

"Yes, yes. In the end, we reach him. We come to a big station, crowded with many people. One time I am pushed so I am … separate from my mother, and I shout. Then she is there again, and at last we reach my uncle's house. There we rest. We try to make plan what to do. But my mother … my mother she is so tired. She start to be ill with fever."

Ania was silent then, staring out at the sky. There was another long pause before she spoke again. When she did, her voice had dropped to a whisper. "We could not get the medicine she need. We try to nurse her, to bring down the fever, but she get more and more ill. Not – how do you say? – not talking sense. And all the while people in my uncle's village are leaving, taking their things…

"After my mother die, and we bury her. My uncle say it is not safe for me to stay longer with him. He fear the same soon happen in his village as happen to us. So he find people who take me, with many other children, on another train. This one called Kindertransport. We cross frontiers. A long, long journey. And I come here, at last, to Liverpool. I stay in many places. And now I am here. With Miss Mellor."

Ania stopped talking and turned her face abruptly towards Joan. There were no tears in her eyes.

"I tell you all this," she said. "You are the first person here in this place I tell. Because you are kind to me. You and your friend and your mother also. You are not like Angela Travis. Or Miss Mellor."

Joan hesitated. Then, awkwardly, she put an arm around Ania's shoulders. But Ania did not respond. She simply stood there, looking back at the watery horizon, which was now very dark.

CHAPTER 14

Ania hardly spoke again on their way back to Ashchurch Avenue. They said goodbye at the corner, and Joan listened to her footsteps echoing past the neat privet hedges, then heard her knock at Miss Mellor's front door, which opened cautiously to admit her into a dim hall.

As Joan walked slowly home, she was thinking a lot about Ania: about the terrible experiences she had been through and her bravery at putting up with her current situation. Joan felt much closer to her now that she had heard her story, and was rather ashamed that she had not taken more trouble to befriend her before.

Joan had always been able to take the security of family life for granted – the in-jokes, the occasional rows and jealousy, people around to chat to in the evenings and back you up when things went wrong. She could hardly imagine what life would be like without it.

She reached home only just in time before the air-raid siren started. Another raid on Liverpool tonight. And, as though a visit from the Luftwaffe wasn't bad enough, Captain Ronnie Harper Jones was in the front room again, chatting to Mum. Joan managed to slip past without being spotted. Being treated to another airing of Ronnie's views on refugees and foreigners in general was more than she could stand after her conversation with Ania.

The bombing was particularly ferocious that night. All the family lay awake until the early hours listening to the ack-ack guns and the barrage of explosives pounding the Liverpool docks.

Next morning they all slept late, and got up exhausted to find that a letter from Dai had arrived for Audrey. As usual, she clutched it tightly and ran upstairs to her room to read it in private. A long time passed before she reappeared with tear-stained cheeks to tell them the news. Dai had posted the letter just before being sent back to sea again without shore leave.

"Not even twenty-four hours!" Audrey moaned. "He'll be at sea again by now. But he says he's going to think about me a lot when he's on night watch, and he'll write as soon as he can and post the letter when his ship docks, wherever that is. The name of the port will be censored, anyway, of course..." Her voice trailed off and she looked so forlorn that none of them knew what to say to comfort her.

"Keep writing back, anyway," Mum suggested, as cheerfully as she could. "And, look, why don't you drop over to see Dai's mum and dad today? I'm sure they could do with a bit of company, and they'd love to see you. You could take them some of the cake that's left over from the tea I made yesterday for Ania."

"If Ronnie Harper Jones hasn't scoffed it already," said Brian bitterly.

Mum ignored this.

It was Saturday morning and Joan's turn for collecting salvage again. As she was standing by the gate, waiting for Ross and Derek to turn up with the handcart, she wondered if she should ask Ania to join them. She was just thinking that they might walk over

111

to Miss Mellor's when Doreen and David came past.

"Guess what!" said Doreen. "Ross and Derek went out on their bikes last night, right in the middle of the air raid! They did it for a dare – cycled all the way up to the top of Bidston Hill and watched the incendiary bombs falling on Birkenhead docks!"

"Crikey!" said Joan. "Their mums must have had a fit."

"Ross's mum was. She was worried stiff. Derek's mum was out somewhere and didn't find out until afterwards." Doreen paused briefly, exchanging looks with Joan. They all knew the rumours about Derek's mum, which were darkly hinted at by the catty gossipmongers who gathered for coffee at the Bluebell Cafe. Rumours the children were not supposed to hear, about how she went out to dance halls in the evenings with servicemen who were stationed locally while Derek's dad was away serving in the army. Derek was often left alone at home, even when there was an air raid.

It was a local scandal, never to be mentioned in the presence of the young, but, of course, they all knew about it. Joan seethed with anger on Derek's behalf – they all did – and admired the way he maintained his air of cocky nonchalance in spite of everything.

"Talk about brave!" said David. "I wouldn't have had the nerve to go out in an air raid like that. But I'll bet it was exciting!"

The three of them walked in silence up the road and hovered on the corner.

"Perhaps they won't be coming today," Joan said hopefully – she hated collecting salvage. But within minutes, there they were – Ross and Derek, trundling their handcart behind them as usual, but perhaps with an extra hint of a swagger. They parked the cart beside the pavement and paused to light up a couple of cigarettes, taking their time and keeping their audience on tenterhooks.

"Tell us what *happened*!" said Doreen. "Did you really go out in the middle of the air raid?"

"Yeah. It was great," said Derek. "We could see the Jerry bombers overhead and all – and the flares. They were hitting the docks, all right. Fires everywhere."

"You're *crazy*!" said Doreen. "You could have been killed."

"Nah." Derek blew out a ring of smoke and looked at her out of the corner of his eye, carefully registering the impression he was making. "We were up on Bidston Hill. The bombs weren't aimed anywhere near us. Well, not *very* near. But the noise was terrible, from the explosions and all – and the warehouses were burning."

"We'd have stayed longer, only the air-raid warden came up and chased us off," Ross told them. "Livid, he was. Thought he was going to burst a blood vessel. Shouted at us. Told us to get off home sharpish and stay in the air-raid shelter until the all clear went!"

"And did you?" Joan asked.

"Yup. But we had a scare on the way home, all right."

"It was dead spooky," said Derek. "Pitch-dark because of the blackout. Couldn't even have our bicycle lamps on either. And we were passing some bombed-out warehouses – weren't we, Ross? – where there was a whole lot of rubble and broken glass thrown across the road. And that was where we saw them."

"Saw what?" Doreen asked.

"Bodies. Lying all over the road. Some with no heads. Arms and legs all over the place."

Joan felt herself go cold with fear. She silently reached for Doreen's hand.

"Bodies?" murmured David. "How do you mean *bodies*? Were they all dead? Why wasn't the ambulance there?"

"No one was there," said Derek. "Everything was still. None of them moving. I've never seen a dead person before, especially not in bits like that. We didn't know what to do, did we, Ross?"

"Scared me, I can tell you!" said Ross. "So we thought we'd better double back and tell the air-raid warden. He came along with us really quick as soon as we told him. But when we got back there, we were in for another shock."

"What? What happened?" Joan urged.

"They weren't stiffs. Not dead people at all."

"Not *dead*?"

"Not *real*! Not live people. It was a clothing warehouse that had been blown up, see," said Ross. "And all the clothes dummies – those models they put up in shop windows – they'd all got blown out in pieces all over the road."

Ross paused to enjoy the sharp intake of breath and stunned silence that followed. Very slowly, Joan released her pressure on Doreen's hand.

"My mum was doing her nut in when I got home,

115

I can tell you!" he said. "But we're going to try it again if we can, aren't we, Derek? Beats trying to get to sleep in a smelly air-raid shelter any time!"

CHAPTER 15

As the autumn term advanced, yet another cloud loomed on Joan's horizon: the school party and dance, an event at which they were to be joined by the boys from the grammar school.

"It's meant to give us all a thrill, I suppose," said Doreen gloomily. "I only hope they don't try to make us do ballroom dancing. Having my feet trampled on by Ross or Derek isn't my idea of a treat."

Angela Travis and her friends were getting very excited about what they were going to wear. Angela was boasting about a new dress that her relatives in America had sent her, together with four pairs of nylons – a huge triumph, intended to make everyone in the class green with envy.

"What will you be wearing, Ania?" she asked sweetly, knowing very well that Ania only had her school uniform and whatever hand-me-down clothing the WVS had managed to find for her.

"Oh, shut up, Angela," said Doreen. "I don't suppose anyone'll notice what any of us wears."

Slowly, the main feeling in the class was turning in Ania's favour. They were all sick of Angela's bullying tactics during break time and her insufferable gloating. But only Joan knew Ania's real story, and how lonely she was at Miss Mellor's.

She decided to make a drawing for Ania, a funny picture of a grinning crocodile emerging from a half-open door with two little legs sticking out of his jaws. She wrote a rhyme to go with it:

"A fussy old lady named Mellor,
Kept a crocodile down in the cellar.
She said, 'It's all right –
I feed him at night!'
But whatever has happened to Mellor?"

When Joan gave it to Ania at school the following day, Ania scrutinized it in silence for a long while.

Then, very slowly, a tiny smile appeared at the corners of her mouth. Then she began to laugh. Ania was actually laughing! A small, stifled, timid laugh, but a laugh nonetheless.

Things are looking up, thought Joan.

The build-up to the school dance involved a lot of serious preparation. They practised the foxtrot up and down the school gym to strict tempo dance music played on a wind-up gramophone operated by their gym mistress, who also called out the steps: "Slow, slow, quick, quick, slow! Now a reverse turn at the corner..."

Joan's problem – as this was an all-girls grammar school – was that the big, tall girls like her had to take the man's part. Wheeling a smaller, daintier girl along while counting the steps under your breath was a feat that demanded maximum concentration. Joan wondered how on earth you were supposed to manage – if you ever actually got invited onto a dance floor by a male partner – to make the necessary light conversation as well as resist the urge to propel him firmly backwards.

The event was scheduled for late afternoon,

rather than evening, to avoid the blackout and the possibility of an air raid. They were let off school early that day to allow time to change out of uniform into their best dresses. Doreen had come up trumps by producing a really pretty dress for Ania to wear – very pale blue to set off her dark hair – as well as a pair of shoes that fitted her and even some precious nylons. At first Ania was reluctant to try them on. But when at last they persuaded her to change, and helped her loosen her hair out of the tightly wound braids and combed it back into a ponytail, the effect was a huge improvement.

The grammar-school boys arrived promptly at four-thirty by bus or on bicycles. Sandwiches and soft drinks had been laid out in the school hall, where eagle-eyed members of staff were hovering. This was clearly going to be a heavily policed event. Grammar-school girls were not supposed to talk to the boys on their way to and from school, or outside the school gates. This invested boys with a glamour that they might not otherwise have had.

Sometimes, in the mornings, as they cycled past (they were experts at riding with no hands on the handlebars), one of the boys would flick a screwed-up note at a girl. This struck Joan as rather romantic. But more often than not the messages she picked up said something like "Tell Doreen Russell I want to take her to the pictures next Saturday. I'll see her outside the Queensway at 6.30" – which was disappointing, though not so much that Joan was ever going to let it spoil her friendship with Doreen.

Now, shambling warily into the school hall, the boys showed less bravado than when they were on their bicycles. They herded sheepishly together on one side of the hall, loitering and jostling about in groups and attempting to appear nonchalant, while the girls chatted self-consciously on the other side.

The atmosphere relaxed slightly after the boys had tucked into the refreshments. Then the music started up and they all looked nervous again. It was up to the boys to ask the girls to dance. *Imagine having to do that and then getting turned down,* thought Joan.

Mind you, it was equally daunting being a girl. What if no boy wanted to dance with you? There was no worse fate than to be stranded as a wallflower, waiting in vain to be invited onto the dance floor. Better to dance with another girl.

Some boys flunked the whole thing from the

outset. This included Ross and Derek, who somehow managed to melt into the background and finish up what was left of the tea. Brian, on the other hand – to Joan's utter astonishment – strode purposefully across the room and invited a redhead called Joyce Barber to dance. After grasping her firmly, he steered her along in fairly good time to the music, and even negotiated the corner with a nifty reverse turn. *Where on earth did he learn to do that?* thought Joan. *And in front of all these people, teachers included?* She had never seen him at any of the youth-club hops. Clearly he had hidden depths that none of the family knew about.

Doreen, in spite of all her grumbling beforehand, had no shortage of partners. She chatted happily as she quickstepped up and down, watched with some envy by Angela Travis, who was lurking among her cronies at the far end of the hall. No one had invited her to dance, despite her new dress.

Joan glanced around to see if she could spot David. He was chatting to a group of friends, but when he saw her, he waved and came over. "You know I'm not good at this kind of thing," he said. "But are you game to risk it for once?"

He put his arm around her waist, took her right hand in his in the approved manner, then they set off down the hall. He certainly wasn't a good dancer, but Joan was too happy to care. She mustered all her skill to guide him around the floor without appearing too pushy. The music helped. It was a quickstep, so quite a few of the other dancers were falling over their own feet. David laughed a lot.

"I never thought I'd manage that," he said as at last they wound up, breathless, by the tea table. "Thanks a lot, Joan!"

Joan felt that this whole event was working out far better than she had expected. Only Ania, standing alone, stiffly pressed up against the wall, paralysed with shyness, was a reminder of what an ordeal this kind of thing could be for some teenagers.

One day, Joan thought, *perhaps they'll just play music and everyone will be able to get up and dance, whether anyone has asked them or not.* Until then, she reflected, you could always follow Ross and Derek's example and fall back on the refreshments.

CHAPTER 16

The event ended early, well before the air-raid sirens started. The boys melted away into the darkness on their bicycles, and most of the girls were met by a parent. Joan knew that Mum would not be able to manage this, as she was at home, putting Judy to bed. She looked around for someone to walk home with, but Brian seemed to have disappeared, and Doreen and David were seeing Ania back to Ashchurch Avenue. Mum hated Joan to be out alone in the blackout, but it was only a short distance home, and so she set out, walking at a brisk pace.

It was dark now, and the overhanging trees in neighbouring front gardens cast dense shadows onto the pavement. There were, of course, no street lights, and all the houses already had their blackout curtains carefully drawn.

Joan was nearly at her front gate when a figure suddenly stepped out of nowhere and stood right in front of her. It was a man wearing a cap pulled down well over his face.

Joan stopped stock-still, ready to scream out at the top of her voice, but somehow no sound came. She tried to gather all her energy to run past him or to punch him in the stomach – anything to make those last few yards home. But the man made no move towards her. He simply stood there and politely removed his cap, so that she could see him clearly.

"Please," he said, "do not be frightened. I mean no harm. I only want to speak a word to you."

Joan paused, eyeing the distance between him and the gate.

"What do you want?" she asked at last. "I warn you, my mum's in there, and she'll hear me if I scream."

"I only wish to tell you who I am. I am Lukasz – Lukasz Topolski. I am Ania's uncle."

There was a long silence. At first, Joan was too surprised to speak. Then she asked, "Have you been around here before?"

"Yes, I have been here. Many times, to back of your house. I think maybe once, twice, you see me. But I have no wish to frighten you like this. The Polish ladies at the Royal Hotel often speak of your mother – what a kind lady she is. I thought perhaps you help me talk to Ania. But I cannot come here in daytime. Only when dark. Because ... because I fear maybe you have ... visitor? Someone who would see me. Because ... I cannot risk to be seen. But I wish to thank you now. You, your mother, your family. With all my heart. For your kindness to Ania."

"Well, she's a friend," said Joan. "She's in my class at school, and she didn't know anybody when she came, so I asked her to tea. Look, I'd better go indoors and fetch Mum—"

"No – no! Cannot be seen. It is not safe. Just please to tell Ania that I am alive – that her Uncle Lukasz is here, near to her. And that I hope to meet with her one day soon, perhaps."

Before Joan could reply, he pulled on his cap and slipped silently back into the shadows. She heard his footsteps receding softly.

Joan ran indoors.

Judy was already in bed, and she found Mum alone in the back room, drinking a cup of tea.

"Hello, darling," she said. "How did the school dance go?"

Joan brushed aside her question and told her about the unexpected encounter she had just had. "Shall I pass the message onto Ania, then?" Joan asked. She was bursting to tell Ania the wonderful news that her Uncle Lukasz was right here, so close to her. "Just think what this will mean to her, Mum!"

But Mum was more cautious.

"We have no idea whether this man's genuine or not, Joanie," she said. "No proof at all. From what you say, it seems as though he's the man who has been hanging around here recently. But that doesn't make him Ania's uncle. There's only one person who can prove that for certain, and that's Ania.

"But we don't want to put her at risk by going searching for this man – just in case he isn't who he says he is. And if he *is* her uncle, then we must be very careful because as a deserter he could end up in a military prison. So just for the moment, until I can arrange a safe meeting between them here without the Military Police finding out, it might be better if you don't mention this to anyone.Not even Brian or Audrey."

And certainly not to Captain Ronnie Harper Jones, thought Joan to herself.

CHAPTER 17

"That's all we need!" said Ross bitterly. "A kids' party! We're doing the salvage collection, aren't we? Surely that's enough without being expected to spend all Saturday afternoon playing daft games with a whole lot of snotty-nosed kids from Liverpool."

"There'll be a tea, I suppose," said Derek, but he sounded equally gloomy.

Joan was expected to go too, of course. Miss Buckley, the head of the local WVS, had said it was obligatory that she turn up to help, and there was no getting out of it. So, at three o'clock, they trudged down the promenade, without their handcart, expecting the worst.

The local WVS ladies had done their best to

decorate what had once been the Royal Hotel dining room. They had made paper chains to hang along the walls and laid out the tea on trestle tables. The children were already assembled, the little ones rampaging up and down the room, impatient for the party games to begin. A group of older girls stood about, stubbornly resisting any attempt at festivity. The older boys had been taken off to do some football practice in the park.

"I'm so glad you're here," said one of the ladies, greeting Joan, Ross and Derek. "Captain Harper Jones has been extremely generous in providing the tea. He even said he might look in later, if he has time. *Such* a public-spirited man! He does so much for us locally. Now, I think we should have some party games before tea, don't you? What about Musical Bumps? Miss Rudd, will you play the piano for us?"

Miss Rudd struck up briskly. Joan took a couple of the very youngest children by the hand and they bounced up and down enthusiastically until the music stopped, at which point everyone had to fall down on the floor. The last person to fall down was out.

Derek made very sure that it was him, and sloped off to lurk sardonically on the sidelines.

Ross managed to get knocked out second and joined him, while Joan and the others struggled gamely on. Muscial Bumps was followed by Oranges and Lemons, then Squeak, Piggy, Squeak. By the time it came to Hunt the Thimble, Ross and Derek had given up all pretence at jollity, and even Joan had to suppress a desire to keep looking at her watch.

At last tea was announced. But just as the children were all seated and beginning to tuck in, the doors of the room were flung open and in marched an army sergeant and two corporals, wearing the distinctive red on their caps to show they were the Military Police. Mrs Buckley hurried forward anxiously.

"Sorry to interrupt," said the sergeant, saluting, "but we've had orders to search this building."

"Now? But is that really necessary? We're in the middle of a children's party, as you can plainly see."

"It is essential, I'm afraid. We've had a tip-off that the army deserter we're looking for may be hiding here." The sergeant glanced around the room, as if the deserter might be hiding under the piano. "Please carry on. My men will start with the kitchens and storerooms, and then work their way up, floor by floor."

"Only the ground, first and second floors are

in use," Mrs Buckley told him. "The children's dormitories are up there. The top floor and attics are locked up." She beckoned to Basia and Gosia, the two Polish women who were helping with the tea. They stepped forward nervously. "These two ladies from my team live here on the premises. They will show you around."

The sergeant motioned for the two women to lead the way, and he and his men followed them out of the room, watched by wide-eyed, open-mouthed children. Joan was just as curious but managed not to show it.

Tea was resumed, although they could hear heavy military boots tramping about overhead. Then, as the search party reached the locked door leading to the top floor, there was a noisy commotion, with Basia and Gosia wailing and protesting as the soldiers began to break it down.

The tea party had now ground to a halt. Mrs Rudd struck up a cheerful tune on the piano, but no one felt like joining in with another game. Some of the younger children looked anxious, and one of them began to cry.

"Sounds as though they're doing a pretty thorough search up there," said Ross.

Joan was silent. She was remembering something one of the older girls had said, that day when they were collecting salvage, about the top floor being haunted and footsteps echoing overhead at night. Perhaps the rumour had spread, so that suspicion had grown locally and the Military Police had been tipped off. Was this where Ania's uncle had been hiding?

Joan got away from the party as soon as she could and ran all the way home. She needed to tell Mum about this right away.

When Joan got home, Ronnie Harper Jones was in the back room with Mum. Brian was up in his room. He'd presumably decamped to there as soon as he had heard Ronnie's voice in the hall.

"I won't stay long," Ronnie said, taking off his greatcoat. He was in his self-important senior-officer mode. "I just dropped in to tell you the news. The Military Police have at last picked up a strong lead on that deserter fellow who's been hanging around here. They've just finished searching the upper floors of the Royal Hotel, where they discovered signs of recent occupation – a camp bed, some clothing, that kind of thing. They're pretty sure that the two

Polish helpers who live at the hotel are responsible for trying to hide the man."

"I know about the search," said Joan. "I was there. They came when we were trying to have a tea party for the children."

Ronnie ignored this, although Mum looked concerned at the thought that Joan had been caught up in something scary.

"They'll soon catch him now," Ronnie said. "It's only a matter of time. He won't last long sleeping rough in this weather before he's spotted. I don't want to alarm you – just wanted to warn you to be extra careful. Keep your doors and windows locked and, of course, report anything suspicious immediately. Don't worry, we'll have him soon."

"Thank you for coming, Ronnie," was all Mum had to say to that. She paused for a moment, considering her next words. "Especially as we know how busy you must be. We won't keep you now. I'm sure we'll be all right."

CHAPTER 18

At school on Monday morning, Joan waited for a quiet moment in the playground to break the news to Ania that her Uncle Lukasz might have reappeared in her life. She braced herself for the reaction. Ania, usually so restrained and buttoned-down, clutched Joan's arms tightly, wide-eyed and hardly able to speak.

"My Uncle Lukasz? Here? Here in this place?" she said at last. "Shall I see him?"

"It's a bit complicated, I'm afraid, Ania. You see, he's wanted by the Military Police – if he *is* your uncle, that is. They think this man has been hiding at the Royal Hotel, but there was a search there and now nobody knows where he is. So, please don't say anything about this at school, or to Miss Mellor, or anyone – not just yet. My mum is trying to help you, to find out if he's genuine. If he only ran away to see you, then he might be able to escape military prison. And you're the one person who can tell us if he really is your uncle."

"Yes, yes. I understand. I am silent. I tell no one," said Ania breathlessly. "But I hope. I so hope."

She took Joan's hands in hers and held them tightly – something she had never done before. "Thank you, thank you! You are true friend. You and your mother and all your family. I trust. I am so…" She could not find the words.

"It'll be OK, Ania," was all Joan could manage to say. And she hoped with all her heart that she was right.

The next couple of days passed without a sign of the man who claimed to be Lukasz Topolski. The Military Police were well in evidence locally, keeping a strict eye on the train and bus stations, the public park and the shelters on the promenade, and asking people to report anything that looked suspicious.

Mum made no attempt to contact them or give them any information. Luckily, no police had actually turned up on the doorstep.

Mum and Joan were sitting alone together late one afternoon, with the curtains already drawn to keep out the sound of the heavy rain falling outside, when they heard a faint whistle and a tap-tapping at the windowpane. Joan froze. It was like a rerun of the spooky moment some months ago when she had first seen that face – Lukasz's face – looking in at her.

Mum got up and went to the back door, put on the safety chain and opened it a crack. Joan hovered behind, peering over her shoulder. There he was. He was unmistakably the same man that she had encountered on her way home from the school dance. He looked terrible: unkempt, exhausted and soaked to the skin. But he removed his cap politely, ignoring the rivulets of rain that were running down his cheeks.

"Madam, I am sorry to frighten you like this. I think you know why I cannot come to your door in the proper way. Your daughter has told you already. I am Lukasz Topolski – Ania's uncle. And I must speak to you."

"It's not safe for you to come here," Mum said. Her voice was remarkably steady, but she was signalling by a gesture of her hand for Joan to keep out of sight.

"I haven't yet told the military authorities about you contacting my daughter. But I warn you that I'll do so immediately, if that becomes necessary."

"Please – please. I beg you not to do that. They will take me soon, anyway. You see, I have come to this country as refugee with no papers. They put me in the British Army Pioneer Corps. As labourer. We do rough work. We dig graves, we mend roads. In Poland, I am skilled man. I have my own business. But I suffer this because I have heard my dear niece Ania is here, alive, somewhere in this area, and I must try to find her. Then we hear our unit will soon be drafted, faraway from this place. So I run away."

"So you *are* a deserter, then?"

"Yes. I know the Military Police are looking for me and it is only a matter of time before they take me. I have nowhere to hide. But my friends – the two ladies who work at the Royal Hotel – they are kind, brave. They know what it is like to be refugee here, how careful you must be not to get in trouble. They help me. They hide me there, on top floor, and give me food. But someone find out. The police come and now I have nowhere to go."

"But surely it would have been better if you had

gone to the proper authorities and asked them to help you to trace Ania?" said Mum.

"No, no. I do not trust. I fear they put me in military prison. That will happen now, anyway – soon, perhaps. But I must see Ania just one time before they take me. Show her that I am alive. Tell her that one day I will come for her, and we will be together. And maybe, when the war is ended, we try to find her father again."

Tears were coursing down his face now, mixing with the rain. "Please. You are kind. Your daughter is friend to Ania. You invite her to your home. You are only people here I trust. Please help me to meet with her just one time. Then you will know that all I tell you is truth."

Mum hesitated. Then she said, "All right. I'll see what I can do. Come back here tomorrow – to the back door – around five o'clock."

Of course, it was no use trying to keep all this from Brian and Audrey, although they managed to avoid letting Judy in on it. The following afternoon, Mum arranged for her to spend the night with their friends, the Hemmings.

"I'll bet you this chap's genuine," said Brian. "Why would he get himself into all this trouble if he wasn't?"

"I hope we'll be able to get this whole thing over before the air-raid siren starts," Audrey commented. "It'll mess up everything if there's an early raid."

Joan knew they were taking a big risk. She felt nervous walking home from school with Ania.

By four-thirty they were all having tea in the back room. Ania was surprisingly calm. After eating, she sat on an upright chair with folded hands, saying very little. Her face was pale, and every bit of her seemed to be alert and listening. Audrey paced up and down restlessly, then turned the radio on. But Brian objected, saying he was trying to get a bit of homework done. Joan hovered about, determined not to show how anxious she was.

At last it came, a faint whistling at the window. Mum got up and went to unlock the back door. They heard low voices, and then she re-entered the room with Lukasz following close behind her.

Ania stood up. There was a moment's silence as she and Lukasz looked at each other. Then she ran forward and put her arms around him. There was no mistaking Lukasz's identity now as they clung silently together, beyond words.

Mum motioned for the family to leave the room and they all stumbled awkwardly to their feet and exited, one by one, into the front room. Ania and Lukasz hardly seemed to notice their departure. They were already talking together in a flood of Polish, crying, laughing and embracing each other by turns.

"What happens now?" Brian asked hoarsely.

"I think we must give them as much time together as we can," said Mum. "But it can't be long. And, to be honest, I don't really know what happens now, Brian. It depends on what kind of plans Lukasz has, if any. But at least we know he's genuine – he really is Ania's uncle, and that's all that matters at the moment."

"Well, I hope they don't take too long over all this tearful stuff," said Brian. "I didn't get time to eat my tea properly, and I'm starving."

"I'll see if—" But Mum was cut off mid-sentence by a loud ring of the front doorbell.

The whole family froze.

"Quick – go and answer it, will you, Audrey?" Mum whispered. "And try to get rid of them, whoever it is. Tell them we're busy. Don't let anyone in, for heaven's sake!"

Audrey scurried to open the door, and to their horror they heard the all-too-familiar voice of Ronnie Harper Jones. After ignoring Audrey's efforts to keep him at bay, he walked straight past her and into the hall.

"Don't want to alarm you again," he was saying, "but the Military Police think they've tracked down this deserter chap at last. It looks as though he may be somewhere in this area, so I came straight over to see that you're all right."

Mum stepped out of the front room and planted herself firmly in his path, blocking the way to the back of the house.

That's brave of her, thought Joan.

"Ronnie! How good of you to come." Her voice sounded high-pitched and louder than usual. "As a matter of fact, we're just having something of a family get-together – not often that we're all home at the same time and there are so many things we need to discuss. I would ask you in, but, as you can see, it isn't the most convenient time..."

"That's all right, my dear. I wouldn't dream of

interrupting you. I'm very pressed for time myself. I just wanted to make sure that—"

Without bothering to remove his greatcoat, he strode past her towards the back of the house. Then he flung open the back sitting-room door.

Ania and Lukasz were standing there, frozen with fear. At the sight of the captain's uniformed figure, Lukasz seemed to crumple. Instinctively, he and Ania both backed away towards the window. Ronnie's ample presence dominated the room. He recognized Lukasz at once, and his moustache positively bristled with triumph.

"Lukasz Topolski?" he said. "Don't bother to deny it. I know who you are. I am a British officer and I am arresting you on a charge of desertion from the army. You will be held in a military prison and face a court martial in due course. The police are in this area and will be here directly, so it is quite useless for you to try to escape. You would be recaptured immediately, believe me."

Lukasz did not reply. He swayed, then steadied himself by holding onto the back of a chair, while facing his captor as bravely as he could. But all his remaining energy seemed to have drained out of him.

He half turned to Ania, who stood transfixed, her eyes wide with fright. He put out his hand towards her in an attempt at reassurance, then let it drop hopelessly to his side.

Ania was in deep shock. Mum, pushing past Ronnie, tried to put an arm around her, but she just stood there, mute, her eyes fixed despairingly on Lukasz. She resisted all attempts to be taken into the front room when the Military Police arrived. It was only when they had put handcuffs on Lukasz and led him away, followed by the triumphant Ronnie, that she broke down and flung her arms over her face in a flood of tears. It was the first time any of them had seen her cry.

CHAPTER 19

Ross, Derek, Joan and Doreen met in a shelter on the prom a day or two later to discuss the whole awful business of Lukasz Topolski's arrest. Doreen knew the most about it because she had overheard some urgent phone calls her father had been making on Lukasz's behalf.

"He's been taken into custody and is awaiting trial, somewhere on the other side of Liverpool," she told them. "He's facing a court martial – that's a sort of military trial – for desertion. And if he's convicted, which is pretty certain, he'll have to serve time in a military prison."

Joan could hardly bear to think about this, knowing what it would do to Ania.

Joan and Doreen had tried calling at Miss Mellor's house in the hope of seeing her, but they were met with a stony response. Miss Mellor had opened the front door a crack, but had resolutely refused to let them have any conversation with Ania. Once they had glimpsed Ania lurking in the hall, but they were not invited in. When she came back to school, Ania was white-faced, turned in on herself, and totally uncommunicative. Even Ross and Derek, who did not usually take much interest in Ania, were despondent.

"Wouldn't much like to be her," said Derek, lighting up and puffing out three perfect smoke rings. "Don't give much for her chances if her uncle's in that sort of trouble."

Joan felt uncomfortable. She knew that her own situation was rather different, because Ronnie Harper Jones had intervened on Mum's behalf and somehow got her involvement in this whole affair kept quiet. Otherwise, Mum might have had to face charges too, for not reporting Lukasz as a deserter to the Military Police and for arranging that fatal meeting at their house.

So, now we're really beholden to Ronnie, Joan

thought gloomily. *He'll be popping by to see Mum all the time, and we'll have to keep on being nice to him.*

The nightly Blitz continued relentlessly, and the weather turned bitterly cold. To Joan, life seemed to have become one dreary round of school, homework, ration queues and long, blacked-out evenings.

There was a brief spell of happiness for Audrey, at last, when Dai turned up on an unexpected week's leave. Security was very tight, and it was an unwritten law that nobody ever enquired where the next voyage would take him when his ship had been refitted. "Careless Talk Costs Lives!" the posters warned.

Mum put her foot down about letting them go dancing in Liverpool in case the bombing started early. But they were too blissfully happy in one another's company to mind much. The local cinemas remained open, and Mum tactfully made the front room available to them, even going to the lengths of lighting a fire in there in the evenings, as well as in the back room – an unheard-of luxury.

But, as always, Dai's leave was over all too soon. After yet another heartbreaking goodbye,

Dai returned to his ship and the perils of the cruel, U-boat-infested North Atlantic.

Joan's family struggled to return to normal. The freezing fog that rolled in up the estuary in the early mornings was slow to clear, and the house was almost as cold indoors as it was outside. Mum looked into the coal cellar, where supplies were running very low.

"I just don't know when we're going to get hold of another delivery," she said. "I keep ringing Mr Williams the coal merchant, but he just says he can't keep up with the demand in the run-up to Christmas."

They all wore their overcoats indoors as well as out and crouched shivering over a tiny fire in the back room in the evenings.

"Some of the boys at school told me that there's a lot of driftwood lying about on the sand hills near the old windmill," said Brian. "I could go there on Saturday and bring some back on my bicycle, and we could dry it out for firewood. It's not much, but it'll save a bit of coal."

"I'll come," said Joan, glad to get out of having to collect salvage.

Early the following Saturday morning, they set

off into the mist, with baskets on both the back and front of their bicycles.

"I feel like Good King Wenceslas," said Brian.

It was quite a long ride, but at least they were glowing with warmth by the time they reached the straggly line of pine trees that fringed the estuary shore. The Old Mill had been a local landmark but was now deserted. It stood in a small clearing above the tideline, enclosed by barbed wire, its rapidly decaying sails standing out starkly against the sky. The storage sheds were equally dilapidated. In happier times, Mum said, people might have made an effort to preserve it, but there was no chance of that now. It would be considered a waste of valuable resources and manpower. There was a stern notice on the fence, which read: PRIVATE PROPERTY. KEEP OUT! TRESPASSERS WILL BE PROSECUTED BY ORDER OF THE MINISTRY OF DEFENCE.

But Brian had been right about the driftwood. There was plenty of it lying about above the tideline on the sand hills, easily enough to fill their bicycle baskets. By mid-morning, they were tired but triumphant.

"This should keep us warm for a while, anyway,"

Brian said. "But I'm *starving*! I wish we'd brought some sandwiches."

"Let's go back," said Joan.

They secured their bundles firmly and set off, pedalling briskly along the bumpy track. The mist was clearing a little, giving way to a soaking drizzle.

They were not far from the road when a van suddenly appeared out of nowhere, heading towards them very fast. It made no effort to slow down as it approached, and Joan and Brian were forced to swerve sharply, to avoid being run over, and ended up in the hedge. Brian shouted some very rude words, some of which were new to Joan, but the van was already out of earshot.

"Did you get his number plate?" said Brian.

"No chance."

"What do you think he's doing, going at that speed right out here? This track doesn't lead anywhere – only the mill. It's just sand hills after that. I'd like to give him a punch on the nose."

"How did you know it was a 'he'?" said Joan. "It might have been a 'she'. The sort of lady driver that Ronnie Harper Jones is always complaining about."

"Well, he can't talk, can he? He gets driven

everywhere in an army car with unlimited petrol and a sweet little ATS driver."

"The bundles stayed on, anyway," said Joan, feeling shaken. "Let's get on home before they get too wet."

It was nearly dinnertime when they arrived back. They found Ronnie talking to Mum by the chilly fireplace. He was in full dress uniform with an impeccably polished Sam Browne belt because, as he explained, he had just come off parade.

"The Catering Corps may not be a combative unit," he told them for the umpteenth time, "but I like to think we can turn out as smartly as any guards regiment when it comes to it. I hear you two have been out collecting firewood for your mother? Well done!"

"At least we'll be able to keep the back room warm this evening," said Mum.

"I only wish I could get you a delivery of coal," Ronnie said. "But, as you know, I never pull strings. It wouldn't be fair on the rest of the civilian population. So I'm delighted to see that you two are doing your bit."

He spoke cheerfully, as though he had forgotten

all about the last occasion he had visited their house and his involvement in Lukasz Topolski's arrest. He had clearly decided not to mention it or anything about the forthcoming court martial for the moment.

Thank heavens Mum isn't going to get into trouble, thought Joan. But she still found Ronnie irritating.

Brian simply ignored him. "Will dinner be ready soon, Mum?" was all he said.

CHAPTER 20

Joan saw very little of David these days, except sometimes on his way to school, when he always waved.

"He's working ever so hard for this scholarship," said Doreen gloomily. "It's making him really edgy. And he isn't sleeping well. I woke up in the middle of the night, long after the all clear had gone, and heard him roaming about downstairs. When I crept down to see what he was doing, I found him taking all the tinned stuff out of the kitchen cupboards."

"Perhaps he was looking for a snack?"

"That was the weird thing. He was just taking them out and looking at the labels, then putting them back again. And when I asked him what he was doing, he snapped my head off."

"Well, we've all got food on the brain at the moment," said Joan. "I know I have. I dream about cream buns and chocolate cake."

Joan's own school work was slipping badly. The only *A*s she got were for art. She found it hard to concentrate on the other subjects when there was so much anxiety about Lukasz, who was still on remand and awaiting trial for desertion. They all knew that things would go badly for him if he were convicted and sent to a military prison.

Joan tried to make Christmas cards, but it was difficult to conjure up a festive image. Judy was the only person in the family who was entering wholeheartedly into the Yuletide spirit, making endless lists of all the things she wanted.

"Poor Judy," said Mum sadly. "I can't bear to think how terribly disappointed she is going to be. I can't possibly manage to get her any of these things – even if they were on sale in the shops."

Even salvage was in short supply. Joan, Ross and Derek continued to do their rounds with the handcart, but people had very little to give. Everyone was burning any combustible rubbish they had to keep warm. Things had also been very quiet at the

Royal Hotel since Lukasz's arrest. Some parents had even come to take their evacuated children back to Liverpool, in spite of the Blitz.

Ross and Derek were planning another night sortie.

"You'll freeze to death in this weather," Joan told them.

"Don't care about that," said Ross. "You get warm pedalling, and it's better than being in the shelter."

When Joan ran into them a few days later, they were in a state of high excitement. She was on her way to check up on Ania, but stopped to talk. They had been out to the old mill and, more daringly than Joan and Brian, had somehow managed to prise open a gap in the barbed-wire fence.

"We had a good nose around," said Derek. "It was dark, but we had our torches. The mill's empty, except for the rats. But guess what? We broke into one of the old outbuildings – the main doors all have brand-new padlocks, but we found a loose door at the back – and there was loads of stuff in there!"

"What kind of stuff?" Joan wanted to know.

"Food. Boxes and boxes of it – coffee, sugar, tea, endless tinned stuff. Lots of it with American labels – Spam and that. We didn't dare help ourselves, of course – though my mum would have been thrilled if we had."

"You think it's an army supply warehouse?" asked Joan, although it seemed odd.

"No. We were still in there when a van arrived," said Ross. "No headlights. Came up very slow and quiet. Boy, were we scared! It definitely wasn't any army vehicle."

"Did you see who was driving?"

"Not likely! Lucky for us they didn't spot our bicycles. We dodged off around the back while they were unlocking the main doors and beat it as quick as we could. We reckon it's black market stuff."

Joan felt a stab of icy panic in the pit of her stomach. She knew all about the black market, how it had sprung up as a response to food rationing. It was illegal and unpatriotic to buy and sell goods in this way, but people still did it.

"You shouldn't go up there again," she said. "It's dangerous, whatever it is. Brian and I nearly got run over when we were collecting firewood. You ought to tell someone what you found. A very responsible grown-up. Someone who'll go to the police."

"Maybe," said Derek. "But not just yet. We like a

bit of a mystery, Ross and me. We're not wimps, so we'll keep going up there."

As Christmas approached, anxiety about Lukasz intensified. He was to remain in custody until he came up for trial in the New Year. Ania was white-faced and silent at school.

"Try not to worry too much," was all Joan could say by way of reassurance. "Doreen's dad is working really hard to build up the evidence for his defence."

A week later, the pre-Christmas gloom that had descended on the family was suddenly lifted when Doreen appeared on their doorstep early one morning. She was bursting with excitement to break the good news.

"Guess what! Lukasz's court martial has been deferred – probably cancelled altogether. They're releasing him on compassionate grounds. He'll be able to join his old unit."

"Doreen! What wonderful news!" Mum said. "How on earth...?"

"It was my dad who fixed it," Doreen told them proudly. "He pulled a lot of strings. Talked to high-up military people he knows about Lukasz's background – what a terrible time he and Ania have had – and he convinced them that he's no traitor. That he deserted out of desperation, then tried to make contact with Ania secretly for fear of getting caught."

"So there won't be any black marks against him?" Mum asked.

"No. He'll be back with the Pioneer Corps, but in a clerical job and stationed locally. And, better still, Mum has rallied lots of local support to get Ania moved from Miss Mellor's to a more suitable kind of family. They've got three kids, one about her age, so she'll have a much better chance of improving her English."

"That should cheer her up no end," said Joan. "She's been walking around at school like some sort of ghost since Lukasz was arrested."

The only person who reacted coolly to this news was Ronnie.

"It's awfully decent of John to go to all that trouble for Topolski," he remarked on his next visit. "But I hope it doesn't give a message to my men that the army is going soft on deserters. Otherwise they'll all start thinking they can bunk off any time there's trouble at home."

CHAPTER 21

As Christmas approached, Ronnie called in more and more frequently. Sometimes he brought food to help with the rations, but mostly he came just to laugh and chat with Mum in the front room. Brian made himself scarce on these occasions and Joan went up to her attic studio. But it was so cold up there that she could not do much drawing. The romantic idea of freezing to death in a garret for art's sake was, she decided, very overrated, even if the alternative was having to listen to Ronnie's conversation.

Audrey was spending a lot of time with her friend Pat and loyally writing letters to Dai that she knew might never reach him. There had been none from him for some weeks, but that was not unusual when he was at sea. He was not a great letter writer at the best of times. When they did arrive, they came in batches, and were lovingly read by Audrey over and over again.

One evening, after tea, when the whole family was gathered together in the back room, Mum turned off the radio and faced them rather self-consciously.

"There's something important I want to tell you. As we're all at home and the air-raid siren hasn't gone yet, this seems like a good time to do it. The thing is... Well, I don't suppose it'll come as much of a surprise..." She paused for a second and cleared her throat. "The thing is, Ronnie has asked me to marry him."

There was a long, strained silence. On one level this was clearly not a surprise, but on another, it was a bombshell.

"It won't be for a while yet," said Mum, talking rather more rapidly than usual. "We want to give you plenty of time to get used to the idea, of course."

"Will this mean he'll be coming to *live* here?" said Audrey.

"Well, no. Not yet, anyway. He's a serving officer, don't forget, so he will still be based at the Catering

Corps headquarters. So nothing will change much for the time being, though naturally he'll want to spend as much time here as possible."

Judy, at least, was pleased. "Oh, goody! Will you have a white dress and a veil and flowers? Will I be a bridesmaid? Where will he sleep? Will he share with Brian? P'raps he'll drive me to school sometimes in his army car!"

The others said nothing. Audrey bent over her unfinished air letter, doodling around the edge with her pen. Joan tried to think of something to say and failed. Brian simply got up and left the room.

After the door had closed behind him, Mum said, "I know how hard it is for you to accept this all at once, and I don't expect you to. We've managed here on our own for so long now, all of us, missing Dad terribly – and you've been brave and wonderful.

"And I know Ronnie hasn't shown up very well in your eyes recently," Mum went on. "He's well aware of how upset you all were by the whole Lukasz affair – but he was only doing his duty as an officer. And that whole business has been resolved happily now, thank goodness. The thing is, he's much more nervous of you lot, when he comes over here, than you realize. He tends to cover up the fact that he's keen for you to like him with too much chat. But he has many good qualities you don't know about – his generosity, for one thing—"

"If he thinks he can bribe his way into our good books by bringing us all this off-ration foodstuff, he's on the wrong track," Joan cut in. "I know it's great having it. But I'm beginning to think I'd rather put up with rationing like everyone else."

Mum got up. "I know just how all of you feel about this. I'm only too well aware of your feelings. But you've got to try and understand how *I* feel too. How tired I am. How sick of trying to keep everything going on my own. I heard someone down at the Home Office propaganda section going on about everyone trying to 'keep calm and carry on', or something like that. Well, I'm trying to. I do so want someone who will put me first – who loves me enough to look after me, and keep me company. I'm just asking you to give him a chance, at least. To try to—"

At that moment, her words were cut short by the familiar sound of the air-raid siren beginning its menacing nightly wail.

It was a mercifully short raid for once, and

afterwards the family discussion was not resumed. Mum was upstairs reading to Judy, Audrey had returned to her letter writing, and Brian was at the kitchen sink, grimly doing the washing up. It was not a task he usually did without being asked. Joan picked up the drying-up cloth, and they worked together for a while in silence.

Then Brian muttered savagely, "I just won't be able to stand it!"

"Stand what?" said Joan, although she knew very well what he meant.

"That chap. That Ronnie actually *living* here. Married to Mum! How can she bear the thought of it?"

"She told us why – you just left before she could explain," said Joan. "About how lonely she is and stuff."

"But he's a *creep*! It's bad enough having him dropping in all the time, hogging the fire in the front room and boring everyone stiff with his awful conversation. Imagine what it'll be like if he actually moves *in*!"

Joan could imagine, all too clearly.

"I know one thing," said Brian. "If Mum goes through with this, I'm moving out. I'm going. I'm not living under the same roof as him!"

"But you can't, Brian. Where would you go?"

"I dunno. I haven't thought yet. But I'll find somewhere. Perhaps if I offer to help look after refugees or evacuees, they'll let me live in some kind of hostel or something."

"But what about your school work? Your exams?"

"I'll manage. Anyway, I'm going to join the Merchant Navy as soon as they'll take me."

Joan went on silently drying the dishes. There seemed to be nothing left to say.

CHAPTER 22

It was not much of a Christmas. Nobody expected it to be. Only Ania was transformed, radiant now with happiness. She had moved into her new billet, where she could see Lukasz whenever he was free. "They are kind and friendly. They invite Lukasz to family dinner on Christmas Day," she told Joan. "We make plans. We talk about my father. How we might find him when the war is over."

"I do hope so, Ania," said Joan.

At home, no one mentioned Mum and Ronnie's engagement. Luckily, Ronnie was on duty on Christmas Day, so they were spared his presence and spent it quietly together.

On Christmas morning, the whole family attended

early service at church, where special prayers were said for servicemen and -women serving abroad and at sea. Then it was time for present-giving.

Mum had found gifts for everyone: two pairs of nylons for Audrey, a special bicycle repair kit for Brian, a beautiful doll wearing an old-fashioned crinoline dress (lovingly made by two old ladies) for Judy, and a pack of watercolour paints and two new brushes for Joan.

The children all had presents for Mum too, mostly purchased in local jumble sales. Mum was especially pleased with Joan's gift. Joan had painted a picture for her and put it in a nice old gilt frame that she had found in the attic. It was an illustration from *Cinderella*, of the moment when Cinders runs from the ballroom, leaving her glass slipper behind. Mum hung it in the front room right away.

Mum had done her best with Christmas dinner too, and they all pitched in to help with the cooking. It was difficult to resist Ronnie's contributions when they were all so hungry. Even Joan's resolve weakened when it came to the Christmas pudding and mince pies.

But by far the best occasion of this not-very-festive season came on New Year's Eve, when the whole family were asked to spend the evening at the Russells'. Ronnie was not invited.

The Russells' lounge was as warm and welcoming as always, with a good fire and holly and mistletoe everywhere. Mr Russell had opened two good bottles of wine for the grown-ups.

"It's the last of a case I brought over from France. Just before the war," he said. "Those were the days… What a long time ago it seems now!"

They all laughed, chatted and gossiped as Mrs Russell handed round some delicious food. Even David, who was usually rather quiet, was in tremendous form. *He's so funny,* Joan thought. Meanwhile, Doreen was tactful enough not to show off all the lovely presents she had received.

One of the best things about this family, thought Joan, *is that they never rub in how much better off they are than us.*

When midnight came, Mr Russell proposed a toast. "To 1941," he said. "And to peace!"

"To peace!" they all cheered, and raised their glasses.

*   *   *

It was a forlorn hope. The festive atmosphere, such as it was, faded very quickly in January, when the Liverpool Blitz intensified, with devastating damage to buildings and docks, and terrible civilian casualties.

Food shortages were worse than ever and Joan felt hungry all the time. She hated running errands for Mum because of the long queues that formed outside any shop rumoured to have a consignment of fish or meat. Sausages were occasionally on offer, but were filled with some dubious substance that certainly wasn't pork. And, although it didn't affect Joan directly, the sight of the pubs closing early, displaying a sign saying, "Sorry, no beer", was dispiriting to local morale.

But Mum explained that it was the Ministry of Food's job to see that nobody starved. "Rationing's awful, but it's all worked out to keep us healthy, if not well fed. At least we've got plenty of fresh vegetables, with everybody digging for victory and all those Land Army girls working flat-out on the farms."

All the same, the meagre sweet ration involved an agonizing choice between scoffing the lot in one go and then going without for the rest of the month, or eking it out, bit by bit. Joan usually preferred the former.

"At least you're all growing up with good strong teeth," said Mum.

Mum like many other self-sacrificing mothers, had long ago declared that she had never really liked chocolate, and divided her rations among the rest of the family.

The post-Christmas gloom was reinforced by headlines in the newspapers and on the radio about the iniquities of the black market. The news reports reeled at the scandal of all kinds of off-ration food being sold at extortionate prices to those who could afford it and were unpatriotic enough to buy it. The stories hinted at corruption in high places: "Not only 'spivs' selling illicitly on street corners, but a canker running right through our society, which must be rooted out!"

Joan's heart sank when she read this, thinking about the old mill, and Ross and Derek's discovery when they were nosing around there.

"You've just got to tell someone about it soon," she told them when they were next out trundling the handcart. "Even if it does get you in trouble for trespassing."

"We're planning just one more trip out there next time there's an air raid on," said Ross. "Might even be able to pick up a bit of stuff."

"You can't do that! It'd be *stealing*!" Joan said.

"No one'll miss it. It's probably all hot, anyway," Derek said.

"You ought to tell someone," Joan repeated.

"Who would we tell?" said Derek. "The police? And have them coming round and asking questions and worrying my mum stiff?"

"Couldn't you tell a grown-up? Someone you can trust?" said Ania, who had started to help them with the collections.

"Don't know anyone," said Ross.

Joan cast about for a suggestion. Ronnie Harper Jones came into her head, but she immediately dismissed it. Things were already complicated enough in that direction. And she would never forget the officious way he had barged into their back room on that terrible evening when he had handed Lukasz over to the Military Police. If it had not been for Mr Russell's timely intervention, Lukasz would be in a military prison by now.

Then a thought struck her. It was so blindingly

obvious that she could not think why it hadn't come to her before. "What about Mr Russell?" she said. "Couldn't you get Doreen or David to tell him about the old mill? He was so great about getting Lukasz's court martial quashed. He'd know what to do."

"OK. We might think about it," said Ross, non-committal as ever.

But a few days later, disaster struck.

It was Ross who broke the bad news to Joan.

"Derek's been in hospital," he told her.

"*What?* Is he ill?"

"Nah. He's got a broken collarbone. Been knocked off his bike. But he's home again now. I've just been to visit him."

"Where did it happen?"

Ross looked slightly shifty.

"Out by the old mill," he said. "We bicycled out there again for another look around. Maybe get some stuff. But we never took anything in the end. Too risky, like you said. It was getting dark and we were on our way back, cycling along that narrow track, when a great lorry with no lights came up behind us out of nowhere! Going like hell, really fast. Drove right at us, deliberately trying to run us down. I managed to swerve into the hedge, but it knocked Derek flying and drove on. He hit the ground hard and broke his collarbone."

"Oh, Ross! That's *terrible!*"

"I didn't get their number plate. I was too busy trying to help Derek. He was really bad, crying with pain and that. I did like they tell you in the first-aid classes – didn't try to move him, but propped his head up a bit and put my jacket over him. Then I beat it out of there as quick as I could to the call box on the main road, near the end of the track, and rang for an ambulance. They took ages – they're short-staffed cos of the air raid and that – but they came in the end."

"Did you tell them that it was a hit-and-run? That someone tried to knock you down on purpose?"

"Nah. We're keen to keep quiet about it, Derek and me. We've agreed we don't want anything to do with the cops. I told them we were riding without lights and that we never had time to get the lorry's number plates. So they took the usual statement and told us off – and now with any luck they'll leave us alone."

Joan, Ania and Doreen went to visit Derek and

took him some of Ronnie's precious chocolate biscuits, left over from Christmas. They found him remarkably cheerful. One good thing at least had come out of this accident.

"My mum's stopped going out in the evenings," he told them. "She's been staying at home with me since I had this bad shoulder. She cried when she came to see me in hospital and said she felt awful that she wasn't there when they rang to tell her. Course, this means it's going to be trickier for Ross and me to get out on our bicycles at night when my shoulder's better. But it's nice having her around, cooking my supper and all."

CHAPTER 23

Soon after this disaster, a banner headline appeared in the local newspaper: BLACK MARKET SCANDAL! ILLICIT FOOD HOARD DISCOVERED!

The front page described how, following reports of dangerous driving out by the old mill, the police had investigated the adjoining premises and found a substantial amount of illicit foodstuffs, including tea, sugar, coffee and all kinds of tinned goods, believed to be destined for the black market.

"'No arrests have yet been made,'" Mum read aloud to them over breakfast one morning, "'but Detective Inspector Walker, who is in charge of the case, promises swift action.'"

The article went on to report that this was part of

a major ongoing investigation into the widespread criminality of black market trading throughout the whole of the Liverpool area.

As a cheerless January wore on, accompanied by the relentless Blitz, it was depressingly obvious that Ronnie was becoming a more or less daily feature of the front room when he wasn't on duty. The topic of his engagement to Mum had been tactfully sidelined for the time being, but Brian made it clear that he could not bear to be in the same room as him, and Joan turned up the radio in the back room whenever he called. Audrey retired upstairs. Only Judy, eager for sweeties, remained loyal.

The gloom of early February was temporarily lifted by the war news that the Allies had made huge advances in the fighting in North Africa, driving Italian and German forces back westwards across the desert. Thousands had surrendered and been taken prisoner. It was a boost to public morale, but it seemed miles away from the grim immediacy of life in north-west England and the day-to-day slog of simply keeping going.

Then, gradually and without any explanation,

a change seemed to take place in the Armitage household. It was hardly noticeable at first, but it was increasingly apparent that Ronnie's visits were becoming rather less frequent, and when he did call by, he seemed less inclined to bring gifts of food. Mum offered no explanation, except to vaguely mention how busy he was at the camp. The rest of the family – except Judy – were relieved that they didn't have to make themselves scarce every time they heard his step in the hall, and this easily compensated for the lack of goodies.

"Why doesn't Ronnie come and see us any more?" Judy kept asking.

"He's got an awful lot of work to do at the moment," Mum said.

The rest of the family, who recognized a lame excuse when they heard one, tactfully kept quiet.

The news, when it came, was like an unexploded bomb that nobody had expected to go off. It took them all completely unawares but was around the district in no time: Captain Ronnie Harper Jones, a senior officer in the Army Catering Corps, had been summoned to give evidence before a civil tribunal that had been tasked with looking into local black market activities. As yet there was no accusation against him personally, but rumours and innuendoes were rife, especially in the Bluebell Cafe. Joan heard the women gossiping when she went in there with Doreen one Saturday afternoon.

"I always thought he was such a charming man – though you can't always go by appearances..."

"I know. He was terribly generous about contributing to our charity auction in aid of war orphans."

"Of course, I *never* buy anything on the black market – well, hardly ever. I mean, I'd have to be *desperate*! It's just not patriotic, is it? And I'm sure Captain Harper Jones has only been asked to shed light on some of the suspicious things that have been happening locally..."

"That awful business of all the stuff they found out at the old mill! Terrible to think that kind of thing could be happening right under our noses!"

In public, Mum put on a brave face, but she looked very tired. She never went to the Bluebell Cafe anyway, but now avoided it like the plague.

Joan felt helpless. She tried to avoid hearing gossip at school. Angela Travis, who was in her element with this kind of situation, went in for a great deal of whispering in corners with her friends. At home, the subject of the inquiry was still being ignored by tacit agreement.

Mum now saw very few friends, and rarely went out except to take Judy to and from school and to do her Red Cross work. But Mrs Russell dropped in from time to time, relaxed and friendly as ever. She never gossiped or talked about the tribunal, just provided a little cheerful company and an occasional exchange of books. Doreen was equally tactful. Joan wondered how she could possibly manage to face school every day without her.

Brian was the only member of the family who remained in excellent spirits. As far as he was concerned, the collapse of the family's already minimal social life was a very small price to pay for not having to hear Ronnie's braying voice in the front room every evening.

When at last the tribunal came to an end, the findings were ambivalent. It was announced that, although there was irrefutable evidence of local black market dealings on a small scale, as yet the jury could not prove any definite connections with the criminal gangs involved with the hoard at the old mill. They were still at large and thought to be Liverpool-based. However, some charges were being made against three clerks at the town hall, who had been selling forged ration books. Captain Harper Jones of the Army Catering Corps, who had for some time been stationed locally, was to be temporarily relieved of his post, pending further investigations.

"You could tell he was fishy a mile off," said Brian triumphantly. "I only wish we hadn't accepted all that stuff off him."

"It wasn't much," said Joan forlornly. "I mean, not like all that stash they found down at the old mill. I can't believe Derek and Ross found it first. We should have told someone."

"Doesn't matter. Everyone knows about it now. All the kids at school are talking about it. It's in the papers and on the local radio."

The whole family tiptoed around the subject until Mum brought it up at last.

"I know you're all wondering about Ronnie," she said. "About our engagement and everything. And I've hated you having to put up with all the gossip at school. I feel utterly responsible and miserable that any of you should have to be dragged into it. But I'll tell you one thing, I wish with all my heart that I'd never accepted any of the food that Ronnie gave us, and if he is culpable, he'll have to answer for it in due course. But I'm not going to completely abandon him now he's in trouble. To be so shamed locally when he has always been popular and respected is a terrible thing to happen to anyone."

"Carrying loyalty a bit far, isn't she?" Brian commented sourly after she had left the room.

"You know Mum." Audrey sighed.

CHAPTER 24

Soon after the tribunal ended, Ronnie came to the house, and he and Mum remained immersed in deep conversation in the front room for a long time. None of the family knew what was being discussed, and Mum clearly had no intention of telling them.

"It'd be typical of Mum to stick with this wretched engagement in spite of him being in trouble," said Audrey.

"Even if he gets moved out of the area?" Joan asked. "They wouldn't be able to see much of each other then."

"People get separated all the time these days. It doesn't make them any less fond of each other," Audrey said, and then added sadly, "I ought to know."

She had recently turned down a couple of invitations to dances from local admirers who were home on leave, even though staying in every Saturday evening, writing letters to Dai and longing for replies, was making her increasingly short-tempered with the rest of the family.

Several weeks passed and they saw no more of Ronnie. It was Joan who inadvertently witnessed the final, totally unexpected blow that changed everything.

She and Mum were setting out to the shops early one Saturday morning to queue for the family rations when a woman neither of them recognized planted herself firmly in their path. Joan had spotted her before, strolling up and down on the other side of the road and glancing up at their house. She was about Mum's age, plump, carefully made-up and very smartly dressed.

"Excuse me. You're Mrs Armitage, I believe?"

Mum stopped and smiled. "Yes. Have we met before?"

"No. I'm not from this area. My house is in Aldershot. But I've been staying here for a few days at the Rockview, a private hotel near the promenade."

She paused. Mum waited encouragingly. "I believe you and your family have been very hospitable to my husband since he's been stationed here," the woman went on, looking them both carefully up and down.

"Your husband?"

"Yes. Ronnie. Captain Ronnie Harper Jones. I am Mrs Harper Jones."

There was a stunned silence. Joan tried hard to melt into the background as she watched a slow flush creeping up Mum's neck. The woman shot a beady glance at her, then turned back to Mum.

"Won't you come into the house?" said Mum faintly. "A cup of coffee, perhaps?"

"No. No, thank you. I'm just on my way back to the hotel to pack. I'm catching the train home from Liverpool this afternoon. I just wanted to thank you for the hospitality you've extended to Ronnie while he's been stationed here. He and I are separated, as you know. I'm Catholic, so there has never been any question of divorce. And now, since all the recent trouble he's had, being summoned before the tribunal and everything, I've decided to give our marriage another chance. His next posting will be quite near to my home, so he will be able to join me when he can at weekends. Make a fresh start, as it were."

She was looking hard at Mum with a fixed smile, carefully calculating the effect her words were having. Joan edged closer to Mum, wishing that the ground would open and swallow them both.

After another long pause, Mum cleared her throat and said, "Of course. I'm sure he'll be greatly missed here. He's done such a lot of good work locally..." Then she faltered into silence.

There was a gleam of triumph in the woman's eyes. She was affable now, as though she had scored a very satisfactory goal.

"Well, I must be on my way..."

"Are you sure we can't offer you—"

"No, really. I shall miss my train if I don't hurry. I just wanted to express my appreciation to you personally. Kindness means *such* a lot in these difficult times."

She cast one more glance at Joan, then offered her hand to Mum. "Goodbye. I'm so glad I was able to meet you." A brief handshake, one last look, then she turned and walked briskly away, her high heels tapping on the pavement.

For a moment, Joan thought Mum was going to

faint. The flush had drained from her face and she was very pale. She took Joan's hand and they both stood there for a while in silence.

"Come on, Mum. Let's go back indoors and I'll make you a cup of tea," Joan said. Together, arm in arm, they walked slowly back to the house.

CHAPTER 25

That was the end of Ronnie.

His departure was very discreet. As soon as his transfer came through, he was replaced by a brisk younger officer, Captain Fletcher, who was reported to be taking the local black market situation very seriously indeed.

"What *bliss* that we're never going to see Ronnie again," Audrey said when she, Brian and Joan were gathered together around the fire in the front room, revelling in having it all to themselves. "How could he possibly have thought that he could ever get away with being engaged to Mum when he had a wife already?"

Brian was in the highest of spirits. "What a break!

186

The best thing that's happened since the Battle of Britain. I always knew that chap was as bogus as a soya sausage, but it never crossed my mind that he was *married*!"

"Perhaps he was banking on telling Mum when she had finally accepted him," said Audrey. "Then, when he had got the ring on her finger, he would have put her through the whole messy business of waiting for him to get unhitched from his previous missus. Poor Mum. It's just so humiliating for her. Thank heavens nobody locally knows, so there won't be any poisonous gossip. We mustn't mention any of this to anyone, not even our closest friends. And we must keep it from Judy or she might go and let the cat out of the bag."

Mum was clearly too upset to talk about it, even to them. The one saving grace was that none of their friends, not even the Russells, seemed to have got wind of the existence of Mrs Harper Jones. It seemed that she had been tactful enough not to make her brief visit known to anyone except Mum. And having scored a bull's-eye, she had returned to Aldershot in triumph.

This was a great relief to Joan. The thought of

such a hot item of gossip hitting the Bluebell Cafe or being circulated at school was too horrific to be contemplated.

Joan could imagine only too well what a meal Angela Travis and her gang would make of it. But she kept remembering Mum's words to them when she broke the news of Ronnie's proposal – about how lonely she felt sometimes, and how much she longed for somebody to look after her. That situation looked as though it was going to be an ongoing certainty now.

Joan was impressed by how brave Mum could be. This was borne out in the following weeks after Ronnie's departure, when she made herself go out and about locally, chatting to neighbours and other parents at the gates of Judy's school. The family tried to do likewise. Judy gradually got tired of asking why Ronnie didn't come round and bring her sweets any more, and all talk of weddings faded from her mind.

Local rumours about Ronnie and his possible connection with the black market died down surprisingly quickly after he had been transferred. In spite of the impact he had made, all the generosity, the socialising and the charity dances were soon forgotten by the ladies of the Bluebell Cafe.

But the scandal of the black market had certainly not gone away. It was hitting the headlines of all the main newspapers. They revealed that goods were being illegally shifted on an alarming scale from several major ports, one of them being Liverpool, and being sold throughout the country at enormous profit. Joan only glanced at the headlines: STOP THIS SHAMEFUL TRADE! MAJOR CRACKDOWN PROMISED SOON!

She found herself remembering that day when she had been waiting for Audrey near the Liverpool docks and had caught sight of Ronnie's face in the cab of an unmarked lorry. She wondered if he had been transporting food then. If only she'd realized it at the time. But that was all over now. Ronnie had gone from their lives, and she felt it was better to let sleeping dogs lie.

The Blitz was so intensive that even visits to the local cinema were being ruled out by parents in case the building took a direct hit. Sitting cooped up at home every evening, waiting for the siren to go, was wearing a little at the family nerves. They were all on edge, especially Audrey, whose only escape from worrying about Dai was to have interminable

189

telephone conversations with her friends, thus making it impossible for anyone else in the family to take a call. Sometimes during a raid, the line was cut off altogether.

"I don't know how much longer I can stick this," said Doreen gloomily as she and Joan were walking home from school together. "I really wanted to see the new Rita Hayworth film, *The Strawberry Blonde*. You know, it's that American comedy that has absolutely nothing to do with the war or people being heroic. But Mum doesn't want me to go, in case the air raid starts early. It's just *so* boring at home. She's out working, driving her lorry all the time. David does endless schoolwork, and Dad is so busy we barely see him. In fact, he's really bad-tempered these days. He snapped my head off the other day when I was playing some dance music on the radiogram. Told me to turn it off, pronto. He never used to be like that."

"My mum's pretty edgy too," said Joan. "Hardly ever laughs like she used to. She's on her own such a lot these days, and Judy's being an absolute pain, as usual."

"Let's have a get-together after school," said

Doreen. "The whole gang – you, me, Ania, Brian, Ross and Derek, and David, if he can make it. We could scrounge some food."

"Great. Where could we have it?"

"Somewhere on neutral ground. No grown-ups. What about one of the shelters on the prom?"

"But it'd be *freezing!*"

"Not too bad if we keep our coats on. We could bring hot drinks in thermos flasks."

Joan shot a glance at Doreen. She thought how characteristic of her it was to have such a crazy, upbeat idea in the face of general dreariness. She was a wonderful friend, someone who could always be relied on to liven up even the most trivial event with a lot of laughs. She also had the confidence to stand up to bullies or anyone she thought was a "phoney", and, above all, she was truly loyal.

"OK, we could try it," Joan said. "Let's tell the others and try to fix a day."

Ross and Derek took a lot of persuading.

"A bit chilly for a picnic, I should think," Ross said. But when they heard that Brian, David and Ania were all game, and that Doreen might be able to get hold of some cakes, they decided to give it a go.

When the day came, the cutting wind that usually blew in from the estuary seemed to have calmed down a little. Great hordes of seagulls soared and dipped over the shallow pools that the receding tide had left in the mud. There was nobody about.

When Joan arrived with some plastic cups and plates that she had stolen from the attic, she found Ania already there, wrapped up warmly in the winter coat that her new hosts had found for her. It was several sizes too big, and her little face emerged eagerly from the turned-up collar. Ross and Derek were next. They had managed to get hold of some sticky buns. All four of them sat in a row on the less draughty side of the shelter and made desultory conversation while they waited for the others to arrive. As the afternoon light began to fade, Ross and Derek started to get restless.

"Don't think much of this picnic," said Ross. "Looks as though the others aren't going to turn up."

"They've probably found something better to do," said Derek. "Let's eat these buns and clear off!"

Ania was disappointed. "A little while longer, yes? This is like special day for me, to be with my friends, when I am so hopeful that I see my Uncle

Lukasz again soon. It make me so happy."

But almost as soon as she had spoken, Brian appeared, speeding along the deserted pavement on his bicycle. As he flung it down, they could see from the look on his face that he had bad news.

"What's wrong?" Joan asked him anxiously. "What's happened to Doreen and David?"

"They won't be coming," said Brian. "They'll be at home with their mum. It's all over town. Mr Russell's been arrested for selling food on the black market!"

CHAPTER 26

The picnic was abandoned, of course.

The news of Mr Russell's arrest was so sudden, so completely unexpected, that Joan found it more dismaying even than Ronnie's fall from grace. That such a serious allegation should be made against the father of her best friend was shocking. "And such a popular man too," Mum said. "This will send shock waves through the whole community."

Mum explained that Mr Russell was being held for questioning with two other senior executives of the Mersey Docks and Harbour Board, where Mr Russell worked, with regard to black market offences.

In the newspaper it said that a cover-up had been attempted, but "relentless police inquiries" had at last completed the case against them. "Access to transport to and from the docks would have been easy for people in such high authority to arrange," the paper wrote. "A whole network of black marketeers, operating nationwide, is suspected of being involved in the distribution of goods throughout the country."

Joan's first thought, when she heard the news, was for Doreen.

"Do you think I should ring her up?" she asked Mum anxiously.

Mum shook her head. "I don't think you should, not yet, Joanie. They'll be fending off all kinds of unwelcome attention from the press, and may not be answering the phone, anyway."

Doreen missed school for one day. She arrived the following morning looking rather pale but otherwise much as usual. Angela Travis and her gang were awaiting her arrival with gloating triumph. As soon as she walked into the classroom, Angela shot up her hand.

"Well, what is it, Angela?" said Miss Sanderson.

"Please can I have permission to change my desk?"

"Whatever for?"

"Because I don't want to sit next to Doreen Russell. My parents wouldn't like me to mix with someone whose father is in trouble with the law. Someone who may even be a convicted criminal!"

Miss Sanderson's reply was scathing. "Please don't be ridiculous, Angela. You know as well as I do that whatever is happening outside this school is not our concern. You are all here to learn and get on with your work, and not to be influenced by local gossip."

"But my father says—"

"That's quite enough. Now hurry up and get your books ready before the bell goes for prayers."

But everyone knew that this was just an opening salvo. Angela's eyes were gleaming with satisfaction as she sat down. She knew that she only had to wait until mid-morning break time to mount her major assault.

When the bell went, Joan, Doreen and Ania walked out into the playground, arm in arm. Angela and her gang were waiting for them, grouped in a tight huddle. They spread out to stand directly in their path. Everyone else melted away to a safe distance.

"I wouldn't want to be in your shoes, Doreen," Angela began. "We all know you've always thought of yourself as posher than most of us – you and your brother – with your big house and all that. But now your dad's probably going to be sent to prison, things are a bit different, aren't they?"

Doreen lifted her chin up. She remained silent, but Joan felt her arm tremble a little.

"Oh, shut up, Angela," Joan said bravely. "We all know how much you love picking on anyone who's in trouble. It's your speciality, isn't it? Kicking anyone who's already down?"

"Well, all I know is that my mum *and* dad say they'd never stoop to getting things on the black market, let alone dealing in it. They say it's as unpatriotic as you can be. And they don't want me to mix with people who do. I'd be ashamed if it was my dad. We all would. That's why I don't want to sit near someone like Doreen in class."

Before Joan could think of a good enough comeback, Ania suddenly stepped forward. To everyone's surprise, she walked up and stood very close to Angela. When she spoke, her voice was quiet but very clear.

"Perhaps you would wish Doreen to wear a yellow star?" she said. "Something so everyone will know she is too low for you or your friends to sit near? This I have seen done to many people, in Poland, before I come here. Perhaps you would like this to happen here? So you can feel more good about yourself. Mr Russell has bad trouble. So now you want us to forget the good things he has done? Like help my Uncle Lukasz when they want to send him to a military prison? Like find me a good place to live? Like to be always..."

"Generous?" offered Joan.

"Yes, generous. Something you never be, Angela, because you do not know how. And now you want that we all think bad of Doreen and her brother and Mrs Russell too, though we know nothing against any of them? When I come from Poland, I think here will be different. But now I find you and your friends just the same as those who drove us out!"

There was a stunned silence. Nobody at school had ever heard quiet little Ania speak like that before. It took Angela some moments to collect herself. But as she opened her mouth to reply, her voice was drowned out by a rousing cheer from all those bystanders who were within earshot.

* * *

When, at last, school was over for the day, Joan and Doreen trudged home together as they always did. It was their first opportunity to talk privately, but now Joan was at a loss to know what to say.

Finally, Doreen broke the silence. "Thanks a lot for sticking up for me today. You and Ania. It was great what she said about my dad."

"Angela Travis and her rotten lot stink," said Joan. "We all think so. Everyone else in the class was right behind you."

"You were all great. I couldn't have faced it..." She paused, her voice faltering, then she went on. "I just keep worrying about how David managed at his school today. He went in, of course. But he's all buttoned up about it. Won't talk to any of us, not even Mum..." She trailed off miserably.

"You've all got lots of friends, don't worry," Joan said. "Brian will stick up for him."

"But no one will believe that none of us knew Dad was in such trouble, not even Mum. I can't imagine how he managed to keep it all from us, especially her. He's been a lot different since Ronnie Harper Jones got transferred, of course. Bad-tempered, snapping our heads off when we tried to talk to him, acting like he never has before. And at night I could hear Mum crying and him pacing around downstairs. David and I both knew what an awful state Mum was in. It was obvious. But she never let on how worried she was about not knowing what was wrong with Dad. She's very good at keeping up appearances."

Abruptly, Doreen stopped walking and turned away. Joan knew she was crying.

"That's the trouble with this place," Doreen said in a muffled voice, "especially now there's a war on. We're all supposed to keep cheerful – never say if you're having a rotten time. Even when something like this happens, and your dad might get sent to prison and all that spiteful crowd at the Bluebell Cafe can't wait to make mincemeat out of your mum, you have to carry on as usual, as though everything's normal..."

"I know," Joan said with conviction. "I do know, believe me."

The following Saturday morning Mum announced that she was going to invite Mrs Russell for a coffee at the Bluebell Cafe.

"But why the Bluebell?" exclaimed Audrey. "You never go there, Mum. You've always said you wouldn't be seen dead there with that lot. And can you imagine what sort of reception the two of you will get now?"

"That's just why I want to go," said Mum. "Sylvia Russell is my friend, and I want to show that crowd that whatever her husband may or may not be accused of, it will always be the case."

When Saturday morning came, Joan and Doreen insisted on tagging along to give moral support. A silence fell when they all walked in together and sat down at a table near the window. Slowly, conversation among the other customers was resumed. Nobody acknowledged them or offered a greeting. Two women rather abruptly called for their bill, gathered their belongings and left.

When the coffee arrived, Mum chatted gallantly, and Mrs Russell did her best to behave normally. But Joan and Doreen remained helplessly silent.

This was a terrible idea, Joan thought. *But whatever happens, we've got to see it through now, for Mum's sake, if nothing else.* Somctimes she wished that Mum was not such a loyal person. It seemed to land her in so much trouble.

They stuck it out for as long as they could, and

then walked homewards together in silence, subdued by what had happened.

When they got inside, Joan climbed up into her attic studio and sat there, fuming. She had always known that the Bluebell Cafe crowd were a lot of narrow-minded, snobbish old cats, but she had never been on the receiving end of their particular brand of spite before. It was terrible to see Mum and Mrs Russell snubbed like that, and not being able to do anything about it.

"As soon as I'm old enough, and this horrible war is over, I'm getting out of here," Joan muttered. "I don't blame Brian for wanting to, and I will too. I'll run away and go to art school, and never come back except to visit Mum and the family and see the few friends I like. I'll live in an attic, so long as it is as far away from the Bluebell Cafe as possible!"

CHAPTER 27

M_r Russell and his suspect colleagues were released on bail after several days of questioning. It was thought that a big cover-up had been attempted, but nevertheless police enquiries had at last built up a strong case against them.

After he returned home, the whole family withdrew into themselves and were hardly seen socially in the neighbourhood, although Mrs Russell was keeping up her war work. It was David and Doreen who faced the worst ordeal – that of having to turn up at school every day. Joan saw David cycling past their house a couple of times, but he failed to see her. Or, if so, he did not wave.

Then, one day, Joan bumped into him quite by

accident. He was walking Raffles, the family dog, in the lane which led down beside the golf course to the shore. He was trudging along, head down, shoulders hunched, and didn't see her until they were almost face to face.

Joan stopped, at a loss as to what to say. She began with a faltering greeting, but David cut her short straight away.

"Don't worry about trying to say it – about my dad, I mean. I've had rather a lot of it at school, you see. Most of my friends have been very decent about it all. And your mum and all your family have been great." He looked away, and whistled to the dog.

"Doreen's been managing pretty well at school," said Joan lamely.

"Thanks. Thanks a lot for sticking up for her." He paused, and when he looked back at her, she could not help noticing how pinched and pale his face was. "Dad had big debts, you see," he said at last. "We none of us knew, of course. If only he'd told us – or Mum, at least – how bad it was. But he always liked entertaining and stuff. We wouldn't have minded doing without at all, like everyone else, if only he'd asked us to. It never occurred to us. I did think it was a bit weird, all that tinned stuff with American labels in our store cupboard, but I never did anything about it, and neither did Doreen or Mum. We just sort of took it for granted. But those others – the people he was involved with – were in it far deeper. They were a lot more crooked than he was, and a lot more ruthless. But I guess things got so tricky that he couldn't get out, no matter how much he wanted to. What finally finished it – made him sort of collapse in on himself – was when Derek got run down by that lorry, out by the old mill. Dad knew that they were using it to store hot goods, of course. But he couldn't bear to think that he was in with people who could sink so low as to run down a teenage boy on purpose."

He picked up a stick and threw it, and Raffles duly obliged by joyfully retrieving it.

"We'll have to move out of our house, of course," he said at last. "Help pay our debts. Go somewhere cheaper, out of this district probably. I know Mum would like to get away. Avoid all the locals whispering about us every time we go out."

"But what about school? Your Cambridge scholarship?"

"That doesn't matter much any more. I've more or less decided to pack it in, anyway. Join up as soon as I'm old enough."

"But..." Joan began, then stopped, realizing how painful any further discussion on the subject would be for him. Instead, she bent down and fondled Raffles's ears. This revelation about them moving was such a blow that she needed time to digest it. The thought of losing Doreen was almost unbearable.

David put Raffles on his lead.

"Got to be getting back," he said. "I've got lots of sorting out to do."

"You will hang onto your record collection, whatever happens, won't you?"

"Hope so."

"And the piano?"

"Not so sure about that."

She watched him walk away, then set off briskly in the opposite direction. She managed to put a good distance between them before she started to cry.

Saying goodbye to Doreen was far, far worse. The Russells' move was planned for the spring. The "for sale" notice was already up outside their house, and they had found temporary rented accommodation on the other side of Liverpool, where they were more or less unknown – except, of course, to the police.

Doreen was somehow managing to put a brave face on things, at least in public.

"I only hope there's a decent cinema somewhere near there," she said to Joan. "But it won't be much fun going on my own."

"We can talk on the phone. I'll give you a full rundown on what's been showing at the Queensway," Joan replied. "Although I don't suppose I'll be going there often either. It won't be nearly so much fun without you."

"Same here. The only really good thing about leaving is not having to see Angela Travis and her gang ever, ever again."

"You could give her a stink bomb as a goodbye present."

"Good idea. But there's sure to be another Angela Travis at my new school. There's always at least one of her type wherever you fetch up. Ania found that out all right."

"Perhaps it'll be nicer out there. Further away from the Blitz," said Joan.

"Maybe. But I'll miss this place. I've never lived anywhere else, you see. I'll miss our house, and looking out at the muddy old estuary, and my bedroom, and, most of all, my friends – you and Ania and Ross and Derek. Especially you."

"We'll meet in Liverpool," said Joan. "Go to a matinée at the big Odeon cinema, perhaps. They have a cafe there, and a cinema organ, and two feature films with an interval in between. And those usherettes in classy uniforms."

"Sounds great," said Doreen. But Joan could see that her bravery was beginning to crack, and there were tears in her eyes.

They had reached Joan's house now, and hovered by the front gate, both completely lost for words. In the end, Doreen turned and walked away without saying anything, waving casually over her shoulder as she always did, but not looking back.

Brian and David had never been such good friends as Joan and Doreen were, but they had become much closer since the case against Mr Russell had become public knowledge.

"He doesn't want to talk about it," Brian told Joan

while they were washing up. "And I don't blame him. The one thing none of them can bear is all this local gossip. But there's one weird thing I found out. You know when Ronnie was being investigated by the police for being *the* Mr Black Market? Well, it turns out that he was pretty small beer compared with Mr Russell. And David says that Ronnie never split on him, never told them anything that might incriminate him or any of the Russell family. In that respect, at least, he was a loyal friend. So perhaps the old blighter had a bit of good in him after all. Although," he added, "that doesn't rule him out as being the biggest creep in the Western hemisphere in all other respects!"

CHAPTER 28

It was a beautiful spring that year. Even the intensified ferocity of the Liverpool Blitz could not completely spoil it, except, of course, for those brave survivors who had seen their homes wrecked, shops and businesses ruined, friends and relatives killed or injured.

The Russells' departure from the district had been accomplished so swiftly and quietly that hardly anyone noticed the removal van parked in the drive outside their house, and their final exodus. Mrs Russell did call in one last time to say goodbye to Mum; a visit that reduced them both to tears.

For Joan it was a huge relief when the school term ended and the Easter holidays began. She missed Doreen terribly and hated having to turn up to class every day to find her no longer there. She had plenty of other friends, of course, but no one to amble home with after school, or share confidences, or make her laugh as Doreen did.

They spoke on the telephone sometimes.

"It's like a morgue here," Doreen told her. "Pine trees, sand hills, lots of houses with big gates and notices saying, 'Beware of the dog!' We can't very well have one on our gate because Raffles is much too daft and friendly to pick a fight with anything, not even a Nazi parachutist – well, *especially* not a Nazi parachutist."

Their plans to meet in Liverpool were out of the question at the moment. It was far too dangerous, even in the daytime.

Joan spent a lot of time in her attic studio. She was trying her hand at fashion drawing now, much influenced by the effortlessly flowing lines of the drawings that she pored over in old copies of *Vogue*. It was exciting to try to draw the kind of clothes that were now quite impossible to buy, even if she had the money. And if one day in the far future she could afford them, the fashions would certainly have changed by then.

Audrey was so depressed about this situation that she could hardly bear to look at fashion ads. To her, gifts of clothing coupons from generous family members – Mum, mostly – were like manna from heaven. Joan mostly made do with school uniform or hand-me-downs, but she didn't let it bother her unduly.

When the first fine spring weather arrived, so did Lukasz, turning up on their doorstep whenever he had time off, armed with a garden fork and spade. Ania came with him. They both turned out to be natural gardeners, and enthused Mum with the idea of making over the back garden into a vegetable patch.

This required an enormous amount of heavy digging. Mum joined in with them whenever she could, and took to poring over seed catalogues in the evenings. Joan helped, and even Judy did too, pottering about with her bucket and spade. But Ania seemed to know more than any of them about planting and growing. Wearing an old pair of men's trousers and her hair tied up in a scarf, she worked untiringly.

Brian popped out from time to time and looked

on encouragingly, but when it came to joining in on Saturday mornings, he usually seemed to find a pressing need to get on with his homework. And Audrey opted out altogether on account of ruining her carefully preserved nail varnish. Nevertheless, there was a huge sense of achievement when the planting was done and the first green shoots began to appear.

"The carrots seem to be coming up splendidly," said Mum. "Perhaps we could even try for some runner beans?"

"Maybe," said Lukasz judiciously, sipping a cup of tea. "It is possible. We 'dig for victory', as the posters tell us, yes?"

"Oh, yes!"

Dai had only one short leave that spring, and it was over all too soon. Audrey had built up to it with such an intensity of vital choices about hairdos, and what to wear, and whether she could get hold of some really good nylons that when the time came to say goodbye, the aftermath was all the more gloomy. She had taken to playing "Goodnight Sweetheart", sung by Al Bowlly, on her portable gramophone in her bedroom over and over again until the rest of the family were sick to death of hearing it.

"Can't you play some Glenn Miller for a change?" Brian complained. "Or Harry James?"

The trial of Mr Russell was a lengthy one. It was reported in all the national newspapers, but Joan didn't follow it. She and Doreen simply avoided talking about it altogether in their telephone conversations. At last, the proceedings came to an end.

The two main culprits were given a four-year prison sentence, but Mr Russell got off more lightly with two years' imprisonment. Mum said that it was because of his excellent track record and the fact that he'd been such a vital part of the community.

Happily, his punishment was later amended to a suspended sentence, which Mum explained meant that he would be allowed out on parole, providing that he regularly reported to the local police. Mum heard from Mrs Russell that he had since involved himself wholeheartedly in voluntary work, helping to re-house families who had been rendered homeless by the Blitz.

But, according to Doreen, things were very tight for them financially now. "Mum's thinking of doing a secretarial course in shorthand and typing, and giving up her voluntary work to get a paid job," she told Joan. "We need the money really badly. She's never worked in an office in her life, and heaven knows how she'll get on in the typing pool. But at least there are plenty of jobs for women of her age now, because so many younger women have gone into the services."

"You'll have to get your own tea now, when you come in from school," said Joan.

"David and Dad's too," said Doreen gloomily, "knowing how hopeless they are at knocking up a decent meal, and then blaming it all on rationing. But at least there's one bit of good news. The history teacher at David's new school has persuaded him to try for the Cambridge scholarship after all."

"Oh, good," said Joan. She nearly added, "Give him my love," but then didn't, in case it sounded soppy.

CHAPTER 29

There were no letters from Dai. Every time the postman came, Audrey rushed to the door, but there was nothing for her.

"Don't worry, love," Mum kept saying. "You know how it is. There'll be a big batch arriving soon, I'm sure."

Audrey fretted. She kept in close touch with Dai's parents, but they'd heard no news either.

Joan, Ross and Derek still pushed the handcart occasionally on Saturday mornings, mostly out of habit. It was good to be out doors now, in the last days of April, when the spring sunshine danced over the estuary and even the local ladies, queuing grimly outside the shops, had dispensed with their headscarves and shapeless overcoats and were attempting a more summery appearance.

One morning Ross turned up with a grin on his face. "My dad's been promoted!" he told them proudly. "Made a sergeant! Mum's ever so chuffed! It means better pay and all! And he's due to come home on leave soon."

"That's *great*," said Joan.

"He's being sent down to Dorset on a training course. Then, well, we don't know where he'll be posted. Abroad, maybe. But we'll see him before that."

As Joan walked home for her dinner, she found herself thinking a lot about her own dad and how much she still missed him. She kept a clear picture of him in her mind, helped by his photograph on the front-room mantelpiece. And she could remember all sorts of precious shared moments – like when he played with her, and took them all on picnics (though never to go swimming, because he said he saw enough water at sea to last him a lifetime), and how he could always make everybody laugh.

There weren't too many laughs to be had at home these days. The comedians on the radio worked hard to keep people cheerful. They toured the country, did shows for the workers in munitions factories, getting everyone to sing along. But the effect wore off pretty quickly. She couldn't help envying kids of her age who still had a dad, even an absent one or someone who couldn't live up to the huge standards you set for them when you were little.

Somehow she had felt so much older since that day, only last autumn, when she had heard Lukasz whistling to her in the dark. Such a lot seemed to have happened since then. Now, with Doreen gone and Mum always trying to put on a brave face, and Audrey waiting anxiously for a letter from Dai, Brian was about the only person she could rely on to be consistently cheerful. Nothing seemed to get him down for long, and he was good at really silly jokes.

When Joan arrived home, she was met by a delicious smell of onions frying, so she knew Mum was getting the dinner ready. Perhaps there might even be some lamb chops, as it was Saturday. Audrey was laying the table when the telephone rang and she ran to answer it. It was a brief call.

"That was Dai's dad," she called out to Mum

when she rang off. "He's coming round."

"Hugh Davies? Coming now? It'll be lovely to see him, of course. Is Gwyneth coming too?"

"No, he's coming on his own."

"Perhaps he'd like to stay for dinner," said Mum. And Joan knew that her mind had immediately leapt to wondering if she could make the chops stretch to another person.

"He said he won't be staying long," Audrey told her.

Mum answered the door. When Hugh Davies walked into the back room, they could see from his expression that this was no ordinary social call. He looked shocked, as though somebody had just hit him in the face.

"Come and sit down, Hugh," said Mum. "Is anything wrong?"

Hugh remained standing. "I came to see Audrey especially," he said. "Didn't want to tell her on the phone, see. It's that ... well ... we've had a telegram."

"It's about Dai, isn't it?" Audrey said.

"Yes. I've brought it with me for you to read. It's from the shipping company. We wanted you to be the first to know. It says Dai's ship was sunk in the mid-Atlantic. They were on their way home. Direct torpedo hit from a U-boat. No survivors. They send their deepest regrets."

Audrey sat down abruptly, still clutching the tablecloth, and looked down mutely at the floor. Her face was very pale. Mum quickly went over and tried to put an arm around her, but Audrey shrugged her off. At last, Mum turned to Hugh.

"This is terrible news for you and Gwyneth. I'm so, so, sorry," she said in a low voice. Hugh said nothing, only nodded. There was an agonized silence.

"I can't stay," he said at last. "Got to get back to Gwyneth."

"Of course."

After Mum had seen him out, she came back into the room. Audrey was still sitting there motionless, as though she had been turned to stone.

"Do you think you could give Judy her dinner and take her over to the Hemmings'?" Mum said quietly to Joan. "Brian's out. I'll stay with Audrey."

Joan was too stunned to reply, but she did as she was told. It was only much later, when she got back home, that the news really hit her. Dai was dead.

She could hear Audrey up in her room, crying and crying, great heaving sobs reaching a crescendo, and Mum's voice rising and falling as she tried unsuccessfully to comfort her.

CHAPTER 30

That terrible Saturday evening was one of the worst in their lives. As it grew dark, they heard what sounded like a massive armada of Nazi bombers heading for Liverpool. To Joan, preparing for bed, it seemed like the worst kind of science-fiction nightmare made real, like something out of H. G. Wells.

That night, she and Brian sat huddled in the broom cupboard under the stairs, which was supposed to be the safest place in the house, feeling the walls tremble and shake. Mum was still upstairs, trying in vain to persuade Audrey to join them. At least Judy was relatively safe with the Hemmings. They had an Anderson air-raid shelter in their back garden. Somehow, Mum had never got round to installing one. This was supposed to be a so-called "safe area", after all, but it certainly did not seem like one tonight.

There was no electric light under the stairs. Joan and Brian had their torches but did not want to use them unless it was absolutely necessary, in case the precious batteries ran out. They sat in the dark on upturned boxes, holding hands – something they had not done since they were children. Until now, Joan had always felt fairly convinced that a bomb would not actually fall on them, but tonight she wasn't so sure. Brian was beyond making jokes. But his hand was steady as it gripped hers, and very comforting. It seemed like an eternity before morning came and the all clear sounded.

Audrey was at last persuaded to join them downstairs, and they all sat in the back room, mute with shock. It was Sunday, but no church bells rang. They had been silenced since the outbreak of war, and would only be rung as a warning in the event of an enemy land invasion – something which, so far, had not happened.

That's one thing, at least, to be grateful for, thought Joan grimly.

It was deathly quiet outside: only some faint stirrings among the neighbours as they crept out of their shelters in an attempt to start the day. In Joan's back garden, the air was heavy with smoke and dust. Bits of charred paper and scraps of wood and plaster were blowing over the grass like mottled snow.

Mum had seldom looked so tired.

"I'll make some tea," said Joan.

As they sat there sipping it, Audrey disappeared upstairs again, and came down a little later, very pale, but wearing a freshly ironed blouse and her best black coat and shirt.

"I'm going to church," she announced, "with Dai's mum and dad. I know they'll be attending the service at the Presbyterian chapel this morning to pray for Dai, and I want to be there with them."

"Are you sure you can cope with it?" said Mum. But they all knew that once Audrey had made up her mind to do something, there was no stopping her.

Joan, Mum and Brian were too tired to go with her. Dazed with exhaustion, they slowly attempted to clear up the mess outside and sweep the dust from the front step. They could see a great pall of smoke over Liverpool and a dull red glow from the fires, which were still burning there.

Brian tried their telephone and found it dead.

"I expect the lines are down," said Mum. "Maybe our local telephone exchange is damaged. But they'll get it going again soon, surely." It was a forlorn feeling to be so cut off.

Mum was looking to see what food she could possibly muster for that day's dinner when they heard the explosion. There had been no warning, no air-raid siren sounded, just a huge shuddering crash which shook the walls of the house. They all three stood there, transfixed, listening.

"That wasn't a Liverpool explosion," whispered Mum. "It was right here, in our neighbourhood!"

They ran to the front door. Outside, not far away, they could hear a lot of screaming and shouting, and the sound of an ambulance siren.

"Audrey!" Mum said. "Oh, God! I should never have let her go out!"

She was already dragging on her coat when there was an urgent ringing at the front doorbell. Brian rushed to answer it. It was Mr Roberts from next door.

Mum clutched his arm. "What is it? Whatever's happened?"

"It was an unexploded bomb – must have been dropped last night. Only just gone off. I ran all the way from the warden's post where I was on duty to tell you."

"Where? Where was it?"

"The Presbyterian chapel in Hartwell Road. Badly damaged. Your daughter Audrey—"

"Audrey? Is she hurt?"

"I'm afraid so. Mr Davies too. The ambulances are there now."

Left alone at home, awaiting Mum's return, was a worse ordeal for Joan and Brian than last night's Blitz. It was made even scarier as information slowly came through about the bombing of Liverpool the night before. A neighbour told them she'd heard that more than five hundred planes had flown over the city, dropping a huge barrage of high explosives. Incendiaries had rained down, transforming homes, shops and warehouses into a raging inferno in a matter of minutes.

"They say the water main burst, so the firemen just had to watch while all those shops and homes and public buildings were burned to ruins," she said. "The air-raid wardens and ambulance crews would have been working all night to try and rescue people from the rubble. There must have been so many killed or injured – poor things. It just doesn't bear thinking about."

Brian and Joan ate some bread and cheese that they found in the larder, then sat in the back room trying to read or listen to the radio, but failing miserably. It was impossible to concentrate on anything. They strained their ears, trying to hear what was happening outside, but their whole suburb seemed to be wrapped in an uncanny silence.

It was well after six o'clock that evening when at last they heard Mum's key in the lock. The front door opened and she came in, supporting Audrey, who was on her feet, but only just. She was very pale and her face was stained with tears. Her left arm was in a sling, and her shoulder heavily bandaged. Mum's face looked grey with exhaustion.

"We must get you to bed," she said. "But first – Joanie, put the kettle on and make us all a hot drink, will you?"

Brian helped Mum to settle Audrey in the armchair while Joan made tea.

"We had to wait a long time at the cottage hospital before they could attend to her," Mum explained.

"There were so many other people there who were much more badly hurt. The unexploded bomb had lodged on the church roof last night, and it blew a huge hole in it when it suddenly went off. It was a miracle that the whole roof didn't collapse. The church is a mass of rubble and debris. The ARP people are working there now. Hugh was concussed by a falling brick, and Gwyneth is still with him at the hospital. I'll try to find out how he is as soon as I can." She turned to Audrey. "Oh, thank God you're safe!" she said. "Thank God! Thank God!"

Audrey was clearly in a lot of pain. She huddled in the chair with her eyes closed. But after they had persuaded her to drink some hot sweet tea, she managed a weary little smile, and looked down at what had once been her best skirt.

"Ruined," she said. "And I put it on for Dai. Oh, Mum, my shoulder's hurting terribly..."

"We'll give you some painkillers. You need to rest. You've had a terrible shock, apart from everything else."

"It's Dai. I keep thinking about Dai. It's so hard to believe he's dead."

"Try not to think about anything for the moment,

darling," said Mum. "You've been ever so brave. Now we really must get you to bed."

But Audrey showed no sign of moving upstairs. She just lay back in the armchair and closed her eyes. Two little tears escaped from her closed lids and trickled slowly down her cheeks. Joan and Brian sat there silently, not knowing what to do or say.

They were all still sitting there when the doorbell went – not an urgent summons this time, but a couple of rings. Brian was first to jump up and run to answer it. There was a brief pause, then voices in the hall.

As Brian led the way into the room, his face stunned and contorted with shock, he paused on the threshold. There was somebody behind him, and he stood back to usher him through. It was Dai! Not a ghost, but the real Dai! Exhausted, rather dishevelled, but smiling broadly. Dai, back from the dead.

"Hi, everyone! Couldn't find anyone at our place, so I thought I'd come over here. Seems like Jerry gave you a real pasting last night, so I wanted to check that you're all OK."

CHAPTER 31

It was some time before they could hear the full story of why Dai had been reported dead. First, he had to rush down to the hospital and help to get his mum and dad home in the ambulance. Luckily, Hugh had been judged fit to be discharged, providing he rested and reported for a check-up at an outpatients' meeting the following day. Gwyneth, though unhurt, was totally drained.

When Dai was settled on the sofa in the Armitages' front room, close to Audrey, he told them everything.

"We were torpedoed by a German U-boat, see. They'd managed to sneak into the convoy and let us have it. Our ship had been separated from the others somehow, and we took a direct hit. Trouble is, with a merchant ship, you don't even have proper guns to fire back, let alone a depth charge. We went down within half an hour of the torpedo hitting us – on fire, split in two, straight into the drink."

"I can't remember much about what happened then," Dai went on, "except that it was pitch-dark and I was in the water, hanging onto a bit of wreckage. There was burning stuff everywhere, and people screaming. Thought I was done for, see. Got carried away from the wreck. Cold! I've never felt so cold! I knew that if any of our crew were still alive, they'd be out there in the water somewhere. But I couldn't see them, and I knew that none of us could last long in that temperature—" He paused for a moment, unable to go on. Audrey held his hand tightly.

"The next thing I remember was somebody pulling me out of the water. Swedish, they were – a fishing trawler, way off course. God knows how they spotted me. Hauled me on board. I passed out, but they managed to keep me alive. I think I must have been out for quite a while – shock, exhaustion, all that. But they warmed me up somehow, brought me round. They even had some vodka! The only trouble was, when I was finally able to speak to them, none of us could understand a word the other was saying. I wanted to get them to radio the company, to get a message to all of you that I was safe. But they didn't understand, and I think their radio communication was a bit duff, anyway.

"The miracle was that it turned out they were heading for Whitehaven! Heaven knows what cargo they were carrying. I thought it was better not to ask. But they were great lads. They made a detour and got me to Liverpool. Just my luck that we docked before the siren went for the worst Blitz attack ever! I tried to telephone Mum and Dad from the docks, but all the lines were down, and I knew all the ambulance services were fully stretched. But some brave bloke gave me a lift. There were fires everywhere... I thought I might have got so far, only to be blown up on the last lap home. But we made it. And here I am."

"Here you are!" echoed Audrey, still holding his hand as though she could hardly believe it.

"Oh, Dai, I'm so glad you're home safe," was all Mum said. She was all choked up with tears.

Joan could not help noticing that, for a moment, she glanced up at the photograph on the mantelpiece, of Dad in uniform.

The one who didn't make it home.

EPILOGUE

Joan, Ross and Derek were trundling the handcart along the promenade. It was a perfect June day, and they were not collecting with much conviction. It was more of a routine now, clocking up the required hours of youth service to keep the ladies down at the WVS depot happy.

Ross's dad had been sent to North Africa to fight against the German army in the Western Desert, commanded by General Rommel.

"We don't hear from him that often," Ross told them. "Got a letter the other day, though. It'd been through the censor, of course, so lots of stuff had been blanked out. Most of what was left was going on about how hot it was, and how water's strictly rationed, and how the sand and flies get into everything, especially the food."

"Better than freezing to death, I s'pose," said Derek philosophically. The headlines that week were full of news that Germany had invaded Russia. "They say we're signing a treaty with Stalin. He's quite *something*! Got a much better moustache than Hitler, and all."

Joan found it difficult to envisage the world-war conflict in such simplistic terms. All she felt like doing was enjoying the comparative calm that had settled at home, with Audrey recovering from her injuries and everyone so happy that Dai was not dead after all.

He had been given extended leave, and was now working in the company offices in Liverpool. They knew he would be sent back to sea soon, but for the moment, he and Audrey were seeing a lot of each other, dating and dancing, and blissfully happy in each other's company. Best of all, the ferocity of the Liverpool Blitz seemed to be abating, with no raids as severe as on that terrible night in May.

Joan knew that Mum missed the Russell family as much as she did. But they were planning a get-together – a foursome in Liverpool with Mrs Russell and Doreen – as soon as it seemed safe enough to go there. They might even meet for a slap-up tea at the Adelphi Hotel – a far cry from the Bluebell Cafe!

The days when the Armitage family had to endure Ronnie Harper Jones's braying laugh and boring conversation in their front room seemed quite long past now. Mum had not mentioned him since that humiliating confrontation with his wife, which only Joan had witnessed. It was best forgotten.

And now, this Saturday morning, when Joan returned from her salvage collecting, she heard Mum laughing in the kitchen. It had been a long time since she had heard her laugh like that. Brian, who was supposed to be helping to get their midday dinner, was fooling around as usual, imitating Vera Lynn in his own version of her hit song:

"There'll always be an England!
But living here's a pain.
We're all so sick of rationing
It's driving us insane!
No sweets and no bananas,

No coffee and no beer,
And if we ask for fish and chips
They say 'We've got none 'ere!'"

Judy was dancing around and joining in. "Got none, got none, got none 'ERE!"

Joan's family were not demonstrative on the whole. Mostly they preferred their affection for one another to remain unexpressed. But today Joan threw down her things, marched into the kitchen, and gave them each a hug.

"What's this for, then?" asked Brian.

"Oh, I don't know," said Joan. "Just so glad we're all still around, I guess. But, hey, what's for dinner? I'm starving!"

HERO ON A BICYCLE

A NOVEL BY

Shirley Hughes

HERO ON A BICYCLE

*A stunning novel from one of the world's best-loved
children's writers and illustrators*

Italy, 1944: Florence is occupied by Nazi German forces.
The Italian resistance movement has not given up
hope, though – and neither have Paolo and his sister,
Constanza. Both are desperate to fight the occupation,
but what can two siblings do against a whole army with
only a bicycle to help them?

*"A thrilling and moving tale.
Danger abounds, but so do love and courage.
I enjoyed it enormously."*

Philip Pullman

"A very exciting wartime story."

Judith Kerr

5" 1800